CW00959097

THE WHITE FEATHER

THE WHITE FEATHER

P. G. Wodehouse

SOUVENIR PRESS

Copyright © 1972 by Souvenir Press
All rights reserved
First published by A. & C. Black Ltd.
This edition published 1972 by Souvenir Press Ltd.,
95 Mortimer Street, London, W.1 and
simultaneously by J. M. Dent & Sons (Canada) Ltd.,
Ontario, Canada

No part may be reproduced in any form without
the permission in writing from the publisher
except by a reviewer who wishes to quote brief
passages for the purposes of a review

ISBN 0 285 62073 8

MADE AND PRINTED IN GREAT BRITAIN BY
THE GARDEN CITY PRESS LIMITED
LETCHWORTH, HERTFORDSHIRE
SG6 1JS

To
MY BROTHER
DICK

PREFACE

The time of this story is a year and a term later than that
of *The Gold Bat*. The history of Wrykyn in between these
two books is dealt with in a number of short stories, some
of them brainy in the extreme, which have appeared in
various magazines. I wanted Messrs Black to publish these,
but they were light on their feet and kept away—a painful
exhibition of the White Feather.

P. G. WODEHOUSE

CONTENTS

I

Expert Opinions

"With apologies to gent opposite," said Clowes, "I must say I don't think much of the team."

"Don't apologise to *me*," said Allardyce disgustedly, as he filled the teapot, "I think they're rotten."

"They ought to have got into form by now, too," said Trevor. "It's not as if this was the first game of the term."

"First game!" Allardyce laughed shortly. "Why, we've only got a couple of club matches and the return match with Ripton to end the season. It is about time they got into form, as you say."

Clowes stared pensively into the fire.

"They struck me," he said, "as the sort of team who'd get into form somewhere in the middle of the cricket season."

"That's about it," said Allardyce. "Try those biscuits, Trevor. They're about the only good thing left in the place."

"School isn't what it was?" inquired Trevor, plunging a hand into the tin that stood on the floor beside him.

"No," said Allardyce, "not only in footer but in everything. The place seems absolutely rotten. It's bad enough losing all our matches, or nearly all. Did you hear that Ripton took thirty-seven points off us last term? And we only just managed to beat Greenburgh by a try to nil."

"We got thirty points last year," he went on. "Thirty-three, and forty-two the year before. Why, we've always simply walked them. It's an understood thing that we smash them. And this year they held us all the time, and it was only a fluke that we scored at all. Their back mis-kicked, and let Barry in."

"Barry struck me as the best of the outsides today," said Clowes. "He's heavier than he was, and faster."

"He's all right," agreed Allardyce. "If only the centres would feed him, we might do something occasionally. But did you ever see such a pair of rotters?"

"The man who was marking me certainly didn't seem particularly brilliant. I don't even know his name. He didn't do anything at footer in my time," said Trevor.

"He's a chap called Attell. He wasn't here with you. He came after the summer holidays. I believe he was sacked from somewhere. He's no good, but there's nobody else. Colours have been simply a gift this year to anyone who can do a thing. Only Barry and myself left from last year's team. I never saw such a clearance as there was after the summer term."

"Where are the boys of the Old Brigade?" sighed Clowes.

"I don't know. I wish they were here," said Allardyce.

Trevor and Clowes had come down, after the Easter term had been in progress for a fortnight, to play for an Oxford A team against the school. The match had resulted in an absurdly easy victory for the visitors by over forty points. Clowes had scored five tries off his own bat, and Trevor, if he had not fed his wing so conscientiously, would probably have scored an equal number. As it was, he had got through twice, and also dropped a goal. The two were now having a late tea with Allardyce in his study. Allardyce had succeeded Trevor as Captain of Football at Wrykyn, and had found the post anything but a sinecure.

For Wrykyn had fallen for the time being on evil days. It was experiencing the reaction which so often takes place in a school in the year following a season of exceptional athletic prosperity. With Trevor as captain of football, both the Ripton matches had been won, and also three out of the four other school matches. In cricket the eleven had had an even finer record, winning all their school matches, and likewise beating the M.C.C. and Old Wrykinians. It was too early to prophesy concerning the fortunes of next term's cricket team, but, if they were going to resemble the fifteen, Wrykyn was doomed to the worst athletic year it had experienced for a decade.

"It's a bit of a come-down after last season, isn't it?" resumed Allardyce, returning to his sorrows. It was a relief to him to discuss his painful case without restraint.

"We were a fine team last year," agreed Clowes, "and especially strong on the left wing. By the way, I see you've moved Barry across."

"Yes. Attell can't pass much, but he passes better from right to left than from left to right; so, Barry being our scoring man, I shifted him across. The chap on the other wing, Stanning, isn't bad at times. Do you remember him? He's in Appleby's. Then Drummond's useful at half."

"Jolly useful," said Trevor. "I thought he would be. I recommended you last year to keep your eye on him."

"Decent chap, Drummond," said Clowes.

"About the only one there is left in the place," observed Allardyce gloomily.

"Our genial host," said Clowes, sawing at the cake, "appears to have that tired feeling. He seems to have lost that *joie de vivre* of his, what?"

"It must be pretty sickening," said Trevor sympathetically. "I'm glad I wasn't captain in a bad year."

"The rummy thing is that the worse they are, the more side they stick on. You see chaps who wouldn't have been in the third in a good year walking about in first fifteen blazers, and first fifteen scarves, and first fifteen stockings, and sweaters with first fifteen colours round the edges. I wonder they don't tattoo their faces with first fifteen colours."

"It would improve some of them," said Clowes.

Allardyce resumed his melancholy remarks. "But, as I was saying, it's not only that the footer's rotten. That you can't help, I suppose. It's the general beastliness of things that I bar. Rows with the town, for instance. We've been having them on and off ever since you left. And it'll be worse now, because there's an election coming off soon. Are you fellows stopping for the night in the town? If so, I should advise you to look out for yourselves."

"Thanks," said Clowes. "I shouldn't like to see Trevor sand-bagged. Nor indeed, should I—for choice—care to be sand-bagged myself. But, as it happens, the good Donaldson is putting us up, so we escape the perils of the town.

"Everybody seems so beastly slack now," continued Allardyce. "It's considered the thing. You're looked on as an awful blood if you say you haven't done a stroke of work for a week. I shouldn't mind that so much if they were some good at anything. But they can't do a thing. The footer's rotten, the gymnasium six is made up of kids an inch high—we shall probably be about ninetieth at the Public Schools' Competition—and there isn't any one who can play racquets for nuts. The only thing that Wrykyn'll do this year is to get the Light-Weights at Aldershot. Drummond ought to manage that. He won the Feathers last time. He's nearly a stone heavier now, and awfully good. But he's the only man we shall send up, I expect. Now that O'Hara and Moriarty are both gone, he's the only chap we have who's up to Aldershot form. And nobody else'll take the trouble to practice. They're all too slack."

"In fact," said Clowes, getting up, "as was only to be expected, the school started going to the dogs directly I left. We shall have to be pushing on now, Allardyce. We promised to look in on Seymour before we went to bed. Friend let us away."

"Good night," said Allardyce.

"What you want," said Clowes solemnly, "is a liver pill. You are looking on life too gloomily. Take a pill. Let there be no stint. Take two. Then we shall hear your merry laugh ringing through the old cloisters once more. Buck up and be a bright and happy lad, Allardyce."

"Take more than a pill to make me that," growled that soured footballer.

Mr Seymour's views on the school resembled those of Allardyce. Wrykyn, in his opinion, was suffering from a reaction.

"It's always the same," he said, "after a very good year. Boys leave, and it's hard to fill their places. I must say I did not expect quite such a clearing out after the summer. We have had bad luck in that way. Maurice, for instance, and Robinson both ought to have had another year at school. It was quite unexpected, their leaving. They would have made all the difference to the forwards. You must have somebody to lead the pack who has had a little experience of first fifteen matches."

"But even then" said Clowes, "they oughtn't to be so rank as they were this afternoon. They seemed such slackers."

"I'm afraid that's the failing of the school just now," agreed Mr Seymour. "They don't play themselves out. They don't put just that last ounce into their work which makes all the difference."

Clowes thought of saying that, to judge by appearances, they did not put in even the first ounce; but refrained. However low an opinion a games' master may have—and even express—of his team, he does not like people to agree too cordially with his criticisms.

"Allardyce seems rather sick about it," said Trevor.

"I am sorry for Allardyce. It is always unpleasant to be the only survivor of an exceptionally good team. He can't forget last year's matches, and suffers continual disappointments because the present team does not play up to the same form."

"He was saying something about rows with the town," said Trevor, after a pause.

"Yes, there has certainly been some unpleasantness lately. It is the penalty we pay for being on the outskirts of a town. Four years out of five nothing happens. But in the fifth, when the school has got a little out of hand—"

"Oh, then it really *has* got out of hand?" asked Clowes.

"Between ourselves, yes," admitted Mr Seymour.

"What sort of rows?" asked Trevor.

Mr Seymour couldn't explain exactly. Nothing, as it were, definite—as yet. No actual complaints so far. But still—well, trouble—yes, trouble.

"For instance," he said, "a boy in my house, Linton— you remember him?—is moving in society at this moment with a swollen lip and minus a front tooth. Of course, I know nothing about it, but I fancy he got into trouble in the town. That is merely a straw which shows how the wind is blowing, but if you lived on the spot you would see more what I mean. There is trouble in the air. And now that this election is coming on, I should not wonder if things came to a head. I can't remember a single election in Wrykyn when there was not disorder in the town. And if the school is going to join in, as it probably will, I shall not be sorry when the holidays come. I know the headmaster is only waiting for an excuse to put the town out of bounds.'

"But the kids have always had a few rows on with that school in the High Street—what's it's name—St Something?" said Clowes.

"Jude's," supplied Trevor.

"St Jude's!" said Mr Seymour. "Have they? I didn't know that."

"Oh yes. I don't know how it started, but it's been going on for two or three years now. It's a School House feud really, but Dexter's are mixed up in it somehow. If a School House fag goes down town he runs like an antelope along the High Street, unless he's got one or two friends with him. I saved dozens of kids from destruction when I was at school. The St Jude's fellows lie in wait, and dash out on them. I used to find School House fags fighting for their lives in back alleys. The enemy fled on my approach. My air of majesty overawed them."

"But a junior school feud matters very little," said Mr Seymour. "You say it has been going on for three years; and I have never heard of it till now. It is when the bigger fellows get mixed up with the town that we have to interfere. I wish the headmaster would put the place out of bounds entirely until the election is over. Except at election time, the town seems to go to sleep."

"That's what we ought to be doing," said Clowes to Trevor. "I think we had better be off now, sir. We promised Mr Donaldson to be in some time tonight."

"It's later than I thought," said Mr Seymour. "Good night, Clowes. How many tries was it that you scored this afternoon? Five? I wish you were still here, to score them for instead of against us. Good night, Trevor. I was glad to see they tried you for Oxford, though you didn't get your blue. You'll be in next year all right. Good night."

The two Old Wrykinians walked along the road towards Donaldson's. It was a fine night, but misty.

"Jove, I'm quite tired," said Clowes. "Hullo!"

"What's up?"

They were opposite Appleby's at the moment. Clowes drew him into the shadow of the fence.

"There's a chap breaking out. I saw him shinning down a rope. Let's wait, and see who it is."

A moment later somebody ran softly through the gateway and disappeared down the road that led to the town.

"Who was it? said Trevor. "I couldn't see."

"I spotted him all right. It was that chap who was marking me today, Stanning. Wonder what he's after. Perhaps he's gone to tar the statue, like O'Hara. Rather a sportsman."

"Rather a silly idiot," said Trevor. "I hope he gets caught."

"You always were one of those kind sympathetic chaps," said Clowes. "Come on, or Donaldson'll be locking us out."

II

SHEEN AT HOME

On the afternoon following the Oxford A match, Sheen, of Seymour's, was sitting over the gas-stove in his study with a Thucydides. He had been staying in that day with a cold. He was always staying in. Everyone has his hobby. That was Sheen's.

Nobody at Wrykyn, even at Seymour's, seemed to know Sheen very well, with the exception of Drummond; and those who troubled to think about the matter at all rather wondered what Drummond saw in him. To the superficial observer the two had nothing in common. Drummond was good at games—he was in the first fifteen and the second eleven, and had won the Feather Weights at Aldershot—and seemed to have no interests outside them. Sheen, on the other hand, played fives for the house, and that was all. He was bad at cricket, and had given up football by special arrangement with Allardyce, on the plea that he wanted all his time for work. He was in for an in-school scholarship, the Gotford. Allardyce, though professing small sympathy with such a degraded ambition, had given him a special dispensation, and since then Sheen had retired from public life even more than he had done hitherto. The examination for the Gotford was to come off towards the end of the term.

The only other Wrykinians with whom Sheen was known to be friendly were Stanning and Attell, of Appleby's. And here those who troubled to think about it wondered still more, for Sheen, whatever his other demerits, was not of the type of Stanning and Attell. There are certain members of every public school, just as there are certain members of every college at the universities, who are "marked men". They have never been detected in any glaring breach of the rules, and their manner towards the powers that be is, as a rule, suave, even deferential. Yet it is one of the things which everybody knows, that they are in the black books of the authorities, and that sooner or later, in the picturesque phrase of the New Yorker, they will "get it in the neck". To this class Stanning and Attell belonged. It was plain to all that the former was the leading member of the firm. A glance at the latter was enough to show that, whatever ambitions he may have had in the direction of villainy, he had not the brains necessary for really satisfactory evil-doing, As for Stanning, he pursued an even course of life, always rigidly obeying the eleventh commandment, "thou shalt not be found out". This kept him from collisions with the authorities; while a ready tongue and an excellent knowledge of the art of boxing — he was, after Drummond, the best Light-Weight in the place—secured him at least tolerance at the hand of the school : and, as a matter of fact, though most of those who knew him disliked him, and particularly those who, like Drummond, were what Clowes had called the Old Brigade, he had, nevertheless, a tolerably large following. A first fifteen man, even in a bad year, can generally find boys anxious to be seen about with him.

That Sheen should have been amongst these surprised one or two people, notably Mr Seymour, who, being games' master had come a good deal into contact with Stanning, and had not been favourably impressed. The fact was that the keynote of Sheen's character was a fear of giving offence. Within limits this is not a reprehensible trait in a person's character, but Sheen overdid it, and it frequently complicated his affairs. There come times when one has to choose which of two people one shall offend. By acting in one way, we offend A. By acting in the opposite way, we annoy B. Sheen had found himself faced by this problem when he began to be friendly with Drummond. Their acquaintance, begun over a game of fives, had progressed. Sheen admired Drummond, as the type of what he would have liked to have been, if he could have managed it. And Drummond felt interested in Sheen because nobody knew much about him. He was, in a way, mysterious. Also, he played the piano really well; and Drummond at that time would have courted anybody who could play for his benefit "Mumblin' Mose", and didn't mind obliging with unlimited encores.

So the two struck up an alliance, and as Drummond hated Stanning only a shade less than Stanning hated him, Sheen was under the painful necessity of choosing between them. He chose Drummond. Whereby he undoubtedly did wisely.

Sheen sat with his Thucydides over the gas-stove, and tried to interest himself in the doings of the Athenian expedition at Syracuse. His brain felt heavy and flabby. He realised dimly that this was because he took too little exercise, and he made a resolution to diminish his hours of work per diem by one, and to devote that one to fives. He would mention it to Drummond when he came in. He would probably come in to tea. The board was spread in anticipation of a visit from him. Herbert, the boot-boy, had been despatched to the town earlier in the afternoon, and had returned with certain food-stuffs which were now stacked in an appetising heap on the table.

Sheen was just making something more or less like sense out of an involved passage of Nikias' speech, in which that eminent general himself seemed to have only a hazy idea of what he was talking about, when the door opened.

He looked up, expecting to see Drummond, but it was Stanning. He felt instantly that "warm shooting" sensation from which David Copperfield suffered in moments of embarrassment. Since the advent of Drummond he had avoided Stanning, and he could not see him without feeling uncomfortable. As they were both in the sixth form, and sat within a couple of yards of one another every day, it will be realised that he was frequently uncomfortable.

"Great Scott!" said Stanning, "swotting?"

Sheen glanced almost guiltily at his Thucydides. Still, it was something of a relief that the other had not opened the conversation with an indictment of Drummond.

"You see," he said apologetically, "I'm in for the Gotford."

"So am I. What's the good of swotting, though? I'm not going to do a stroke."

As Stanning was the only one of his rivals of whom he had any real fear, Sheen might have replied with justice that, if that was the case, the more he swotted the better. But he said nothing. He looked at the stove, and dog's-eared the Thucydides.

"What a worm you are, always staying in!" said Stanning.

"I caught a cold watching the match yesterday."

"You're as flabby as—" Stanning looked round for a simile, "as a dough-nut. Why don't you take some exercise?"

"I'm going to play fives, I think. I do need some exercise."

"Fives? Why don't you play footer?"

"I haven't time. I want to work."

"What rot. I'm not doing a stroke."

Stanning seemed to derive a spiritual pride from this admission.

"Tell you what, then," said Stanning, "I'll play you tomorrow after school.

Sheen looked a shade more uncomfortable, but he made an effort, and declined the invitation.

"I shall probably be playing Drummond," he said.

"Oh, all right," said Stanning. "*I* don't care. Play whom you like."

There was a pause.

"As a matter of fact," resumed Stanning, "what I came here for was to tell you about last night. I got out, and went to Mitchell's. Why didn't you come? Didn't you get my note? I sent a kid with it."

Mitchell was a young gentleman of rich but honest parents, who had left the school at Christmas. He was in his father's office, and lived in his father's house on the outskirts of the town. From time to time his father went up to London on matters connected with business, leaving him alone in the house. On these occasions Mitchell the younger would write to Stanning, with whom when at school he had been on friendly terms; and Stanning, breaking out of his house after everybody had gone to bed, would make his way to the Mitchell residence, and spend a pleasant hour or so there. Mitchell senior owned Turkish cigarettes and a billiard table. Stanning appreciated both. There was also a piano, and Stanning had brought Sheen with him one night to play it. The getting-out and the subsequent getting-in had nearly whitened Sheen's hair, and it was only by a series of miracles that he had escaped detection. Once, he felt, was more than enough; and when a fag from Appleby's had brought him Stanning's note, containing an invitation to a second jaunt of the kind, he had refused to be lured into the business again.

"Yes, I got the note," he said.

"Then why didn't you come? Mitchell was asking where you were."

"It's so beastly risky."

"Risky! Rot."

"We should get sacked if we were caught."

"Well, don't get caught, then."

Sheen registered an internal vow that he would not.

"He wanted us to go again on Monday. Will you come?"

"I—don't think I will, Stanning," said Sheen. "It isn't worth it."

"You mean you funk it. That's what's the matter with you."

"Yes, I do," admitted Sheen.

As a rule—in stories—the person who owns that he is afraid gets unlimited applause and adulation, and feels a glow of conscious merit. But with Sheen it was otherwise. The admission made him if possible, more uncomfortable than he had been before.

"Mitchell will be sick," said Stanning.

Sheen said nothing.

Stanning changed the subject.

"Well, at anyrate," he said, "give us some tea. You seem to have been victualling for a siege."

"I'm awfully sorry," said Sheen, turning a deeper shade

of red and experiencing a redoubled attack of the warm shooting, "but the fact is, I'm waiting for Drummond."

Stanning got up, and expressed his candid opinion of Drummond in a few words.

He said more. He described Sheen, too in unflattering terms.

"Look here," he said, "you may think it jolly fine to drop me just because you've got to know Drummond a bit, but you'll be sick enough that you've done it before you've finished."

"It isn't that—" began Sheen.

"I don't care what it is. You slink about trying to avoid me all day, and you won't do a thing I ask you to do."

"But you see—"

"Oh, shut up," said Stanning.

III

Sheen Receives Visitors and Advice

While Sheen had been interviewing Stanning, in study twelve, farther down the passage, Linton and his friend Dunstable, who was in Day's house, were discussing ways and means. Like Stanning, Dunstable had demanded tea, and had been informed that there was none for him.

"Well, you are a bright specimen, aren't you?" said Dunstable, seating himself on the table which should have been groaning under the weight of cake and biscuits. "I should like to know where you expect to go to. You lure me in here, and then have the cheek to tell me you haven't got anything to eat. What have you done with it all?"

"There was half a cake—"

"Bring it on."

"Young Menzies bagged it after the match yesterday. His brother came down with the Oxford A team, and he had to give him tea in his study. Then there were some biscuits—"

"What's the matter with biscuits? *They're* all right. Bring them on. Biscuits forward. Show biscuits."

"Menzies took them as well."

Dunstable eyed him sorrowfully.

You always were a bit of a maniac," he said, "but I never thought you were quite such a complete gibberer as to let Menzies get away with all your grub. Well, the only thing to do is to touch him for tea. He owes us one. Come on."

They proceeded down the passage and stopped at the door of study three.

"Hullo!" said Menzies, as they entered.

"We've come to tea," said Dunstable. "Cut the satisfying sandwich. Let's see a little more of that hissing urn of yours, Menzies. Bustle about, and be the dashing host."

"I wasn't expecting you."

"I can't help your troubles," said Dunstable.

"I've not got anything. I was thinking of coming to you, Linton."

"Where's that cake?"

"Finished. My brother simply walked into it."

"Greed," said Dunstable unkindly, "seems to be the besetting sin of the Menzies'. Well, what are you going to do about it? I don't wish to threaten, but I'm a demon when I'm roused. Being done out of my tea is sure to rouse me. And owing to unfortunate accident of being stonily broken, I can't go to the shop. You're responsible for the slump in provisions, Menzies, and you must see us through this. What are you going to do about it?"

"Do either of you chaps know Sheen at all?"

"I don't," said Linton. "Not to speak to."

"You can't expect us to know all your shady friends," said Dunstable. "Why?"

"He's got a tea on this evening. If you knew him well enough, you might borrow something from him. I met Herbert in the dinner-hour carrying in all sorts of things to his study. Still, if you don't know him——"

"Don't let a trifle of that sort stand in the way," said Dunstable. "Which is his study?"

"Come on, Linton," said Dunstable. "Be a man, and lead the way. Go in as if he'd invited us. Ten to one he'll think he did, if you don't spoil the thing by laughing."

"What, invite ourselves to tea?" asked Linton, beginning to grasp the idea.

"That's it. Sheen's the sort of ass who won't do a thing. Anyhow, its worth trying. Smith in our house got a tea out of him that way last term. Coming, Menzies?"

"Not much. I hope he kicks you out."

"Come on, then, Linton. If Menzies cares to chuck away a square meal, let him."

Thus, no sooner had the door of Sheen's study closed upon Stanning than it was opened again to admit Linton and Dunstable.

"Well," said Linton, affably, "here we are."

"Hope we're not late," said Dunstable. "You said somewhere about five. It's just struck. Shall we start?"

He stooped, and took the kettle from the stove.

"Don't you bother," he said to Sheen, who had watched this manoeuvre with an air of amazement, "I'll do all the dirty work."

"But——" began Sheen.

"That's all right," said Dunstable soothingly. "I like it."

The intellectual pressure of the affair was too much for Sheen. He could not recollect having invited Linton, with whom he had exchanged only about a dozen words that term, much less Dunstable, whom he merely knew by sight. Yet here they were, behaving like honoured guests. It was plain that there was a misunderstanding somewhere, but he shrank from grappling with it. He did not want to hurt their feelings. It would be awkward enough if they discovered their mistake for themselves.

So he exerted himself nervously to play the host, and the first twinge of remorse which Linton felt came when Sheen pressed upon him a bag of biscuits which, he knew, could not have cost less than one and sixpence a pound. His heart warmed to one who could do the thing in such style.

Dunstable, apparently, was worried by no scruples. He leaned back easily in his chair, and kept up a bright flow of conversation.

"You're not looking well, Sheen," he said. "You ought to take more exercise. Why don't you come down town with us one of these days and do a bit of canvassing? It's a rag. Linton lost a tooth at it the other day. We're going down on Saturday to do a bit more."

"Oh!" said Sheen, politely.

"We shall get one or two more chaps to help next time. It isn't good enough, only us two. We had four great beefy hooligans on to us when Linton got his tooth knocked out. We had to run. There's a regular gang of them going about the town, now that the election's on. A red-headed fellow, who looks like a butcher, seems to boss the show. They call him Albert. He'll have to be slain one of these days, for the credit of the school. I should like to get Drummond on to him."

"I was expecting Drummond to tea," said Sheen.

"He's running and passing with the fifteen," said Linton. "He ought to be in soon. Why, here he is. Hullo, Drummond!"

"Hullo!" said the newcomer, looking at his two fellow-visitors as if he were surprised to see them there.

"How were the First?" asked Dunstable.

"Oh, rotten. Any tea left?"

Conversation flagged from this point, and shortly afterwards Dunstable and Linton went.

"Come and tea with me some time," said Linton.

"Oh, thanks," said Sheen. "Thanks awfully."

"It was rather a shame," said Linton to Dunstable, as they went back to their study, "rushing him like that. I shouldn't wonder if he's quite a good sort, when one gets to know him."

"He must be a rotter to let himself be rushed. By Jove, I should like to see someone try that game on with me."

In the study they had left, Drummond was engaged in pointing this out to Sheen.

"The First are rank bad," he said. "The outsides were passing rottenly today. We shall have another forty points taken off us when we play Ripton. By the way, I didn't know you were a pal of Linton's."

"I'm not," said Sheen.

"Well, he seemed pretty much at home just now."

"I can't understand it. I'm certain I never asked him to tea. Or Dunstable either. Yet they came in as if I had. I didn't like to hurt their feelings by telling them."

Drummond stared.

"What, they came without being asked! Heavens! man, you must buck up a bit and keep awake, or you'll have an awful time. Of course those two chaps were simply trying it on. I had an idea it might be that when I came in. Why did you let them? Why didn't you scrag them?"

"Oh, I don't know," said Sheen uncomfortably.

"But, look here, it's rot. You *must* keep your end up in a place like this, or everybody in the house'll be ragging you.

Chaps will, naturally, play the goat if you let them. Has this ever happened before?"

Sheen admitted reluctantly that it had. He was beginning to see things. It is never pleasant to feel one has been bluffed.

"Once last term," he said, "Smith, a chap in Day's, came to tea like that. I couldn't very well do anything."

"And Dunstable is in Day's. They compared notes. I wonder you haven't had the whole school dropping in on you, lining up in long queues down the passage. Look here, Sheen, you really must pull yourself together. I'm not ragging. You'll have a beastly time if you're so feeble. I hope you won't be sick with me for saying it, but I can't help that. It's all for your own good. And it's really pure slackness that's the cause of it all."

"I hate hurting people's feelings," said Sheen.

"Oh, rot. As if anybody here had any feelings. Besides, it doesn't hurt a chap's feelings being told to get out, when he knows he's no business in a place."

"Oh, all right," said Sheen shortly.

"Glad you see it," said Drummond. "Well, I'm off. Wonder if there's anybody in that bath."

He reappeared a few moments later. During his absence Sheen overheard certain shrill protestations which were apparently being uttered in the neighbourhood of the bath-room door.

"There was," he said, putting his head into the study and grinning cheerfully at Sheen. "There was young Renford, who had no earthly business to be there. I've just looked in to point the moral. Suppose you'd have let him bag all the hot water, which ought to have come to his elders and betters, for fear of hurting his feelings; and gone without your bath. I went on my theory that nobody at Wrykyn, least of all a fag, has any feelings. I turfed him out without a touch of remorse. You get much the best results my way. So long."

And the head disappeared; and shortly afterwards there came from across the passage muffled but cheerful sounds of splashing.

IV

The Better Part of Valour

The borough of Wrykyn had been a little unfortunate—or fortunate, according to the point of view—in the matter of elections. The latter point of view was that of the younger and more irresponsible section of the community, which liked elections because they were exciting. The former was that of the tradespeople, who disliked them because they got their windows broken.

Wrykyn had passed through an election and its attendant festivities in the previous year, when Sir Eustace Briggs, the mayor of the town, had been returned by a comfortable majority. Since then ill-health had caused that gentleman to resign his seat, and the place was once more in a state of unrest. This time the school was deeply interested in the matter. The previous election had not stirred them. They did not care whether Sir Eustace Briggs defeated Mr Saul Pedder, or whether Mr Saul Pedder wiped the political floor with Sir Eustace Briggs. Mr Pedder was an energetic Radical; but owing to the fact that Wrykyn had always returned a Conservative member, and did not see its way to a change as yet, his energy had done him very little good. The school had looked on him as a sportsman, and read his speeches in the local paper with amusement; but they were not interested. Now, however, things were changed. The Conservative candidate, Sir William Bruce, was one of themselves—an Old Wrykinian, a governor of the school, a man who always watched school-matches, and the donor of the Bruce Challenge Cup for the school mile. In fine, one of the best. He was also the father of Jack Bruce, a day-boy on the engineering side. The school would have liked to have made a popular hero of Jack Bruce. If he had liked, he could have gone about with quite a suite

of retainers. But he was a quiet, self-sufficing youth, and
was rarely to be seen in public. The engineering side of a
public school has workshops and other weirdnesses which
keep it occupied after the ordinary school hours. It was
generally understood that Bruce was a good sort of chap
if you knew him, but you had got to know him first;
brilliant at his work, and devoted to it; a useful slow bowler;
known to be able to drive and repair the family motor-car;
one who seldom spoke unless spoken to, but who, when he
did speak, generally had something sensible to say. Beyond
that, report said little.

As he refused to allow the school to work off its enthusiasm on him, they were obliged to work it off elsewhere.
Hence the disturbances which had become frequent between
school and town. The inflammatory speeches of Mr Saul
Pedder had caused a swashbuckling spirit to spread among
the rowdy element of the town. Gangs of youths, to adopt
the police-court term, had developed a habit of parading
the streets arm-in-arm, shouting "Good old Pedder!" When
these met some person or persons who did not consider Mr
Pedder good and old, there was generally what the local
police-force described as a "frakkus".

It was in one of these frakkuses that Linton had lost a
valuable tooth.

Two days had elapsed since Dunstable and Linton had
looked in on Sheen for tea. It was a Saturday afternoon,
and roll-call was just over. There was no first fifteen match,
only a rather uninteresting house-match, Templar's *versus*
Donaldson's, and existence in the school grounds showed
signs of becoming tame.

"What a beastly term the Easter term is," said Linton,
yawning. "There won't be a thing to do till the house-
matches begin properly."

Seymour's had won their first match, as had Day's.
They would not be called upon to perform for another
week or more.

"Let's get a boat out," suggested Dunstable.

"Such a beastly day."

"Let's have tea at the shop."

"Rather slow. How about going to Cook's?"

"All right. Toss you who pays."

Cook's was a shop in the town to which the school most resorted when in need of refreshment.

"Wonder if we shall meet Albert."

Linton licked the place where his tooth should have been, and said he hoped so.

Sergeant Cook, the six-foot proprietor of the shop, was examining a broken window when they arrived, and muttering to himself.,

"Hullo!" said Dunstable, "what's this? New idea for ventilation? Golly, massa, who frew dat brick?"

"Done it at ar-parse six last night, he did," said Sergeant Cook, "the red-'eaded young scallywag. Ketch 'im—I'll give 'im—"

"Sounds like dear old Albert," said Linton. "Who did it, sergeant?"

"Red-headed young mongrel. 'Good old Pedder,' he says. 'I'll give you Pedder,' I says. Then bang it comes right on top of the muffins, and when I doubled out after 'im 'e'd gone."

Mrs Cook appeared and corroborated witness's evidence. Dunstable ordered tea.

"We may meet him on our way home," said Linton. "If we do, I'll give him something from you with your love. I owe him a lot for myself."

Mrs Cook clicked her tongue compassionately at the sight of the obvious void in the speaker's mouth.

"You'll 'ave to 'ave a forlse one, Mr Linton," said Sergeant Cook with gloomy relish.

The back shop was empty. Dunstable and Linton sat down and began tea. Sergeant Cook came to the door from time to time and dilated further on his grievances.

"Gentlemen from the school they come in 'ere and says ain't it all a joke and exciting and what not. But I says to them, you 'aven't got to live in it, I says. That's what it is. You 'aven't got to live in it, I says. Glad when it's all over, that's what I'll be."

" 'Nother jug of hot water, please," said Linton.

The Sergeant shouted the order over his shoulder, as if he were addressing a half-company on parade, and returned to his woes.

"You 'aven't got to live in it, I says. That's what it is. It's this everlasting worry and flurry day in and day out, and not knowing what's going to 'appen next, and one man coming in and saying 'Vote for Bruce', and another 'Vote for Pedder', and another saying how it's the poor man's loaf he's fighting for—if he'd only *buy* a loaf, now—'ullo, 'ullo, wot's this?"

There was a "confused noise without", as Shakespeare would put it, and into the shop came clattering Barry and McTodd, of Seymour's, closely followed by Stanning and Attell.

"This is getting a bit too thick," said Barry, collapsing into a chair.

From the outer shop came the voice of Sergeant Cook.

"Let me jest come to you, you red-'eaded—"

Roars of derision from the road.

"That's Albert," said Linton, jumping up.

"Yes, I heard them call him that," said Barry. "McTodd and I were coming down here to tea, when they started going for us, so we nipped in here, hoping to find reinforcements."

"We were just behind you," said Stanning. "I got one of them a beauty. He went down like a shot."

"Albert?" inquired Linton.

"No. A little chap."

"Let's go out, and smash them up," suggested Linton excitedly.

Dunstable treated the situation more coolly.

"Wait a bit," he said. "No hurry. Let's finish tea at any rate. You'd better eat as much as you can now Linton. You may have no teeth left to do it with afterwards," he added cheerfully.

"Let's chuck things at them," said McTodd.

"Don't be an ass," said Barry. "What on earth's the good of that?"

"Well, it would be something," said McTodd vaguely.

. .

"Hit 'em with a muffin," suggested Stanning. "Dash, I barked my knuckles on that man. But I bet he felt it."

"Look here, I'm going out," said Linton. "Come on, Dunstable."

Dunstable continued his meal without hurry.

"What's the excitement?" he said. "There's plenty of time. Dear old Albert's not the sort of chap to go away when he's got us cornered here. The first principle of warfare is to get a good feed before you start."

"And anyhow," said Barry, "I came here for tea, and I'm going to have it."

Sergeant Cook was recalled from the door, and received the orders.

"They've just gone round the corner," he said, "and that red-'eaded one 'e says he's goin' to wait if he 'as to wait all night."

"Quite right," said Dunstable, approvingly. "Sensible chap, Albert. If you see him, you might tell him we shan't be long, will you?"

A quarter of an hour passed.

"Kerm out," shouted a voice from the street.

Dunstable looked at the others.

"Perhaps we might be moving now," he said, getting up "Ready?"

"We must keep together," said Barry.

"You goin' out, Mr Dunstable?" inquired Sergeant Cook.

"Yes. Good bye. You'll see that we're decently buried won't you?"

The garrison made its sortie.

It happened that Drummond and Sheen were also among those whom it had struck that afternoon that tea at Cook's would be pleasant; and they came upon the combatants some five minutes after battle had been joined. The town contingent were filling the air with strange cries, Albert's voice being easily heard above the din, while the Wrykinians, as public-school men should, were fighting quietly and without unseemly tumult.

"By Jove," said Drummond, "here's a row on."

2—TWF * *

Sheen stopped dead, with a queer, sinking feeling within him. He gulped. Drummond did not notice these portents. He was observing the battle.

Suddenly he uttered an exclamation.

"Why, it's some of our chaps! There's a Seymour's cap. Isn't that McTodd? And, great Scott! there's Barry. Come on, man!"

Sheen did not move.

"Ought we . . . to get . . . mixed up . . . ?" he began.

Drummond looked at him with open eyes. Sheen babbled on.

"The old man might not like—sixth form, you see— oughtn't we to—?"

There was a yell of triumph from the town army as the red-haired Albert, plunging through the fray, sent Barry staggering against the wall. Sheen caught a glimpse of Albert's grinning face as he turned. He had a cut over one eye. It bled.

"Come on," said Drummond, beginning to run to the scene of action.

Sheen paused for a moment irresolutely. Then he walked rapidly in the opposite direction.

V

The White Feather

It was not until he had reached his study that Sheen
thoroughly realised what he had done. All the way home
he had been defending himself eloquently against an
imaginary accuser; and he had built up a very sound,
thoughtful, and logical series of arguments to show that he
was not only not to blame for what he had done, but had
acted in highly statesmanlike and praiseworthy manner.
After all, he was in the sixth. Not a prefect, it was true,
but, still, practically a prefect. The headmaster disliked
unpleasantness between school and town, much more so
between the sixth form of the school and the town. Therefore, he had done his duty in refusing to be drawn into a
fight with Albert and friends. Besides, why should he be
expected to join in whenever he saw a couple of fellows
fighting? It wasn't reasonable. It was no business of his.
Why, it was absurd. He had no quarrel with those fellows.
It wasn't cowardice. It was simply that he had kept his
head better than Drummond, and seen further into the
matter. Besides . . .

But when he sat down in his chair, this mood changed.
There is a vast difference between the view one takes of
things when one is walking briskly, and that which comes
when one thinks the thing over coldly. As he sat there, the
wall of defence which he had built up slipped away brick
by brick, and there was the fact staring at him, without
covering or disguise.

It was no good arguing against himself. No amount of
argument could wipe away the truth. He had been afraid,
and had shown it. And he had shown it when, in a sense,
he was representing the school, when Wrykyn looked to
him to help it keep its end up against the town.

The more he reflected, the more he saw how far-reaching were the consequences of that failure in the hour of need. He had disgraced himself. He had disgraced Seymour's. He had disgraced the school. He was an outcast.

This mood, the natural reaction from his first glow of almost jaunty self-righteousness, lasted till the lock-up bell rang, when it was succeeded by another. This time he took a more reasonable view of the affair. It occurred to him that there was a chance that his defection had passed unnoticed. Nothing could make his case seem better in his own eyes, but it might be that the thing would end there. The house might not have lost credit.

An overwhelming curiosity seized him to find out how it had all ended. The ten minutes of grace which followed the ringing of the lock-up bell had passed. Drummond and the rest must be back by now.

He went down the passage to Drummond's study. Somebody was inside. He could hear him.

He knocked at the door.

Drummond was sitting at the table reading. He looked up, and there was a silence. Sheen's mouth felt dry. He could not think how to begin. He noticed that Drummond's face was unmarked. Looking down, he saw that one of the knuckles of the hand that held the book was swollen and cut.

"Drummond, I—"

Drummond lowered the book.

"Get out," he said. He spoke without heat, calmly, as if he were making some conventional remark by way of starting a conversation.

"I only came to ask—"

"Get out," said Drummond again.

There was another pause. Drummond raised his book and went on reading.

Sheen left the room.

Outside he ran into Linton. Unlike Drummond, Linton bore marks of the encounter. As in the case of the hero of Calverley's poem, one of his speaking eyes was sable. The swelling of his lip was increased. There was a deep red bruise on his forehead. In spite of these injuries, however, he was cheerful. He was whistling when Sheen collided with him.

"Sorry," said Linton, and went on into the study.

"Well," he said, "how are you feeling, Drummond? Lucky beggar, you haven't got a mark. I wish I could duck like you. Well, we have fought the good fight. Exit Albert —sweep him up. You gave him enough to last him for the rest of the term. I couldn't tackle the brute. He's as strong as a horse. My word, it was lucky you happened to come up. Albert was making hay of us. Still, all's well that ends well. We have smitten the Philistines this day. By the way—"

"What's up now?"

"Who was that chap with you when you came up?"

"Which chap?"

"I thought I saw some one."

"You shouldn't eat so much tea. You saw double."

"There wasn't anybody?"

"No," said Drummond.

"Not Sheen?"

"No," said Drummond, irritably. "How many more times do you want me to say it?"

"All right," said Linton, "I only asked I met him outside."

"Who?"

"Sheen."

"Oh!"

"You might be sociable."

"I know I might. But I want to read."

"Lucky man. Wish I could. I can hardly see. Well, good bye, then. I'm off."

"Good," grunted Drummond. "You know your way out, don't you?"

Linton went back to his own study.

"It's all very well," he said to himself, "for Drummond to deny it, but I'll swear I saw Sheen with him. So did Dunstable. I'll cut out and ask him about it after prep. If he really was there, and cut off, something ought to be done about it. The chap ought to be kicked. He's a disgrace to the house."

Dunstable, questioned after preparation, refused to commit himself.

"I thought I saw somebody with Drummond," he said, "and I had a sort of idea it was Sheen. Still, I was pretty busy at the time, and wasn't paying much attention to anything, except that long, thin bargee with the bowler. I wish those men would hit straight. It's beastly difficult to guard a round-arm swing. My right ear feels like a cauliflower. Does it look rum?"

"Beastly. But what about this? You can't swear to Sheen then?"

"No. Better give him the benefit of the doubt. What does Drummond say? You ought to ask him."

"I have. He says he was alone."

"Well, that settles it. What an ass you are. If Drummond doesn't know, who does?"

"I believe he's simply hushing it up."

"Well, let us hush it up, too. It's no good bothering about it. We licked them all right."

"But it's such a beastly thing for the house."

"Then why the dickens do you want it to get about? Surely the best thing you can do is to dry up and say nothing about it."

"But something ought to be done."

"What's the good of troubling about a man like Sheen? He never was any good, and this doesn't make him very much worse. Besides, he'll probably be sick enough on his own account. I know I should, if I'd done it. And, anyway, we don't know that he did do it."

"I'm certain he did. I could swear it was him."

"Anyhow, for goodness' sake let the thing drop."

"All right. But I shall cut him."

"Well, that would be punishment enough for anybody, whatever he'd done. Fancy existence without your bright conversation. It doesn't bear thinking of. You do look a freak with that eye and that lump on your forehead. You ought to wear a mask."

"That ear of yours," said Linton with satisfaction, "will be about three times its ordinary size tomorrow. And it always was too large. Good night."

On his way back to Seymour's Mason of Appleby's, who was standing at his house gate imbibing fresh air, preparatory to going to bed, accosted him.

"I say, Linton," he said, "—hullo, you look a wreck, don't you ! — I say, what's all this about your house ?"

"What about my house ?"

"Funking, and all that. Sheen, you know. Stanning has just been telling me."

"Then he saw him, too !" exclaimed Linton, involuntarily.

"Oh, it's true, then ? Did he really cut off like that ? Stanning said he did, but I wouldn't believe him at first. You aren't going ? Good night."

So the thing was out. Linton had not counted on Stanning having seen what he and Dunstable had seen. It was impossible to hush it up now. The scutcheon of Seymour's was definitely blotted. The name of the house was being held up to scorn in Appleby's probably everywhere else as well. It was a nuisance, thought Linton, but it could not be helped. After all, it was a judgment on the house for harbouring such a specimen as Sheen.

In Seymour's there was tumult and an impromptu indignation meeting. Stanning had gone to work scientifically. From the moment that, ducking under the guard of a sturdy town youth, he had caught sight of Sheen retreating from the fray, he had grasped the fact that here, readymade, was his chance of working off his grudge against him. All he had to do was to spread the news abroad, and the school would do the rest. On his return from the town he had mentioned the facts of the case to one or two of the more garrulous members of his house, and they had passed it on to everybody they met during the interval in the middle of preparation. By the end of preparation half the school knew what had happened.

Seymour's was furious. The senior day-room to a man condemned Sheen. The junior day-room was crimson in the face and incoherent. The demeanour of a junior in moments of excitement generally lacks that repose which marks the philosopher.

"He ought to be kicked," shrilled Renford.

"We shall get rotted by those kids in Dexter's," moaned Harvey.

"Disgracing the house!" thundered Watson.

"Let's go and chuck things at his door," suggested Renford.

A move was made to the passage in which Sheen's study was situated, and, with divers groans and howls, the junior day-room hove football boots and cricket stumps at the door.

The success of the meeting, however, was entirely neutralised by the fact that in the same passage stood the study of Rigby, the head of the house. Also Rigby was trying at the moment to turn into idiomatic Greek verse the words : "The Days of Peace and Slumberous calm have fled", and this corroboration of the statement annoyed him to the extent of causing him to dash out and sow lines among the revellers like some monarch scattering largesse. The junior day-room retired to its lair to inveigh against the brutal ways of those in authority, and begin working off the commission it had received.

The howls in the passage were the first official intimation Sheen had received that his shortcomings were public property. The word "Funk!" shouted through his keyhole, had not unnaturally given him an inkling as to the state of affairs.

So Drummond had given him away, he thought. Probably he had told Linton the whole story the moment after he, Sheen, had met the latter at the door of the study. And perhaps he was now telling it to the rest of the house. Of all the mixed sensations from which he suffered as he went to his dormitory that night, one of resentment against Drummond was the keenest.

Sheen was in the fourth dormitory, where the majority of the day-room slept. He was in the position of a sort of extra house prefect, as far as the dormitory was concerned. It was a large dormitory, and Mr Seymour had fancied that it might, perhaps, be something of a handful for a single prefect. As a matter of fact, however, Drummond, who was in charge, had shown early in the term that he was more than capable of managing the place single handed. He was popular and determined. The dormitory was orderly, partly because it liked him, principally because it had to be.

He had an opportunity of exhibiting his powers of control that night. When Sheen came in, the room was full. Drummond was in bed, reading his novel. The other ornaments of the dormitory were in various stages of undress.

As Sheen appeared, a sudden hissing broke out from the farther corner of the room. Sheen flushed, and walked to his bed. The hissing increased in volume and richness.

"Shut up that noise," said Drummond, without looking up from his book.

The hissing diminished. Only two or three of the more reckless kept it up.

Drummond looked across the room at them.

"Stop that noise, and get into bed," he said quietly.

The hissing ceased. He went on with his book again.

Silence reigned in dormitory four.

VI

ALBERT REDIVIVUS

By murdering in cold blood a large and respected family, and afterwards depositing their bodies in a reservoir, one may gain, we are told, much unpopularity in the neighbourhood of one's crime; while robbing a church will get one cordially disliked especially by the vicar. But, to be really an outcast, to feel that one has no friend in the world, one must break an important public-school commandment.

Sheen had always been something of a hermit. In his most sociable moments he had never had more than one or two friends; but he had never before known what it meant to be completely isolated. It was like living in a world of ghosts, or, rather, like being a ghost in a living world. That disagreeable experience of being looked through, as if one were invisible, comes to the average person, it may be half a dozen times in his life. Sheen had to put up with it a hundred times a day. People who were talking to one another stopped when he appeared and waited until he had passed on before beginning again. Altogether, he was made to feel that he had done for himself, that, as far as the life of the school was concerned, he did not exist.

There had been some talk, particularly in the senior day-room, of more active measures. It was thought that nothing less than a court-martial could meet the case. But the house prefects had been against it. Sheen was in the sixth, and, however monstrous and unspeakable might have been his acts, it would hardly do to treat him as if he were a junior. And the scheme had been definitely discouraged by Drummond, who had stated, without wrapping the gist of his remarks in elusive phrases, that in the event of a court-martial being held he would interview the president of the same and knock his head off. So Seymour's had fallen back

on the punishment which from their earliest beginnings
the public schools have meted out to their criminals. They
had cut Sheen dead.

In a way Sheen benefited from this excommunication.
Now that he could not even play fives, for want of an
opponent, there was nothing left for him to do but work.
Fortunately, he had an object. The Gotford would be
coming on in a few weeks, and the more work he could do
for it, the better. Though Stanning was the only one of his
rivals whom he feared, and though *he* was known to be
taking very little trouble over the matter, it was best to run
as few risks as possible. Stanning was one of those people
who produce great results in their work without seeming
to do anything for them.

So Sheen shut himself up in his study and ground grimly
away at his books, and for exercise went for cross-country
walks. It was a monotonous kind of existence. For the space
of a week the only Wrykinian who spoke a single word to
him was Bruce, the son of the Conservative candidate for
Wrykyn : and Bruce's conversation had been limited to
two remarks. He had said, "You might play that again,
will you?" and, later, "Thanks". He had come into the
music-room while Sheen was practising one afternoon, and
had sat down, without speaking, on a chair by the door.
When Sheen had played for the second time the piece which
had won his approval, Bruce thanked him and left the
room. As the solitary break in the monotony of the week,
Sheen remembered the incident rather vividly.

Since the great rout of Albert and his minions outside
Cook's, things, as far as the seniors were concerned, had
been quiet between school and town. Linton and Dunstable
had gone to and from Cook's two days in succession without
let or hindrance. It was generally believed that, owing to the
unerring way in which he had put his head in front of
Drummond's left on that memorable occasion, the scarlet-
haired one was at present dry-docked for repairs. The story
in the school—it had grown with the days—was that
Drummond had laid the enemy out on the pavement with
a sickening crash, and that he had still been there at, so to

speak, the close of play. As a matter of fact, Albert was in excellent shape, and only an unfortunate previous engagement prevented him from ranging the streets near Cook's as before. Sir William Bruce was addressing a meeting in another part of the town, and Albert thought it his duty to be on hand to boo.

In the junior portion of the school the feud with the town was brisk. Mention has been made of a certain St Jude's, between which seat of learning and the fags of Dexter's and the School House there was a spirited vendetta.

Jackson, of Dexter's was one of the pillars of the movement. Jackson was

> a calm-brow'd lad,
> Yet mad, at moments, as a hatter,

and he derived a great deal of pleasure from warring against St Jude's. It helped him to enjoy his meals. He slept the better for it. After a little turn up with a Judy he was fuller of that spirit of manly fortitude and forbearance so necessary to those whom Fate brought frequently into contact with Mr Dexter. The Judies wore mortar-boards, and it was an enjoyable pastime sending these spinning into space during one of the usual *rencontres* in the High Street. From the fact that he and his friends were invariably outnumbered, there was a sporting element in these affairs, though occasionally this inferiority of numbers was the cause of his executing a scientific retreat with the enemy harassing his men up to the very edge of the town. This had happened on the last occasion. There had been casualties. No fewer than six house-caps had fallen into the enemy's hands, and he himself had been tripped up and rolled in a puddle.

He burned to avenge this disaster.

"Coming down to Cook's?" he said to his ally, Painter. It was just a week since the Sheen episode.

"All right," said Painter.

"Suppose we go by the High Street," suggested Jackson, casually.

"Then we'd better get a few more chaps," said Painter.

A few more chaps were collected, and the party, numbering eight, set off for the town. There were present such stalwarts as Borwick and Crowle, both of Dexter's, and Tomlin, of the School House, a useful man to have by you in an emergency. It was Tomlin who, on one occasion, attacked by two terrific champions of St Jude's in a narrow passage, had vanquished them both, and sent their mortar-boards miles into the empyrean, so that they were never the same mortar-boards again, but wore ever after a bruised and draggled look.

The expedition passed down the High Street without adventure, until, by common consent, it stopped at the lofty wall which bounded the playground of St Jude's.

From the other side of the wall came sounds of revelry, shrill squealings and shoutings. The Judies were disporting themselves at one of their weird games. It was known that they played touch-last, and Scandal said that another of their favourite recreations was marbles. The juniors at Wrykyn believed that it was to hide these excesses from the gaze of the public that the playground wall had been made so high. Eye-witnesses, who had peeped through the door in the said wall, reported that what the Judies seemed to do mostly was to chase one another about the playground, shrieking at the top of their voices. But, they added, this was probably a mere ruse to divert suspicion. They had almost certainly got the marbles in their pockets all the time.

The expedition stopped, and looked itself in the face.

"How about buzzing something at them?" said Jackson earnestly.

"You can get oranges over the road," said Tomlin in his helpful way.

Jackson vanished into the shop indicated, and reappeared a few moments later with a brown paper bag.

"It seems a beastly waste," suggested the economical Painter.

"That's all right," said Jackson, "they're all bad. The man thought I was rotting him when I asked if he'd got any bad oranges, but I got them at last. Give us a leg up, some one."

Willing hands urged him to the top of the wall. He drew out a green orange, and threw it.

There was a sudden silence on the other side of the wall. Then a howl of wrath went up to the heavens. Jackson rapidly emptied his bag.

"Got him!" he exclaimed, as the last orange sped on its way. "Look out, they're coming!"

The expedition had begun to move off with quiet dignity, when from the doorway in the wall there poured forth a stream of mortar-boarded warriors, shrieking defiance. The expedition advanced to meet them.

As usual, the Judies had the advantage in numbers, and, filled to the brim with righteous indignation, they were proceeding to make things uncommonly warm for the invaders—Painter had lost his cap, and Tomlin three waistcoat buttons—when the eye of Jackson, roving up and down the street, was caught by a Seymour's cap. He was about to shout for assistance when he perceived that the newcomer was Sheen, and refrained. It was no use, he felt, asking Sheen for help.

But just as Sheen arrived and the ranks of the expedition were beginning to give way before the strenuous onslaught of the Judies, the latter, almost with one accord, turned and bolted into their playground again. Looking round, Tomlin, that first of generals, saw the reason, and uttered a warning.

A mutual foe had appeared. From a passage on the left of the road there had debouched on to the field of action Albert himself and two of his band.

The expedition flew without false shame. It is to be doubted whether one of Albert's calibre would have troubled to attack such small game, but it was the firm opinion of the Wrykyn fags and the Judies that he and his men were to be avoided.

The newcomers did not pursue them. They contented themselves with shouting at them. One of the band threw a stone.

Then they caught sight of Sheen.

Albert said, "Oo er!" and advanced at the double. His companions followed him.

Sheen watched them come, and backed against the wall. His heart was thumping furiously. He was in for it now, he felt. He had come down to the town with this very situation in his mind. A wild idea of doing something to restore his self-respect and his credit in the eyes of the house had driven him to the High Street. But now that the crisis had actually arrived, he would have given much to have been in his study again.

Albert was quite close now. Sheen could see the marks which had resulted from his interview with Drummond. With all his force Sheen hit out, and experienced a curious thrill as his fist went home. It was a poor blow from a scientific point of view, but Sheen's fives had given him muscle, and it checked Albert. That youth, however, recovered rapidly, and the next few moments passed in a whirl for Sheen. He received a stinging blow on his left ear, and another which deprived him of his whole stock of breath, and then he was on the ground, conscious only of a wish to stay there for ever.

VII

Mr Joe Bevan

Almost involuntarily he staggered up to receive another blow which sent him down again.

"That'll do," said a voice.

Sheen got up, panting. Between him and his assailant stood a short, sturdy man in a tweed suit. He was waving Albert back, and Albert appeared to be dissatisfied. He was arguing hotly with the newcomer.

"Now, you go away," said that worthy, mildly, "just you go away."

Albert gave it as his opinion that the speaker would do well not to come interfering in what didn't concern him. What he wanted, asserted Albert, was a thick ear.

"Coming pushing yourself in," added Albert querulously.

"You go away," repeated the stranger. "You go away. I don't want to have trouble with you."

Albert's reply was to hit out with his left hand in the direction of the speaker's face. The stranger, without fuss, touched the back of Albert's wrist gently with the palm of his right hand, and Albert, turning round in a circle, ended the manoeuvre with his back towards his opponent. He faced round again irresolutely. The thing had surprised him.

"You go away," said the other, as if he were making the observation for the first time.

"It's Joe Bevan," said one of Albert's friends, excitedly.

Albert's jaw fell. His freckled face paled.

"You go away," repeated the man in the tweed suit, whose conversation seemed inclined to run in a groove.

This time Albert took the advice. His friends had already taken it.

"Thanks," said Sheen.

"Beware," said Mr Bevan oracularly, "of entrance to a

quarrel; but, being in, bear't that th' opposèd may beware
of thee. Always counter back when you guard. When a
man shows you his right like that, always push out your
hand straight. The straight left rules the boxing world.
Feeling better, sir?"

"Yes, thanks."

"He got that right in just on the spot. I was watching.
When you see a man coming to hit you with his right like
that, don't you draw back. Get on top of him. He can't
hit you then."

That feeling of utter collapse, which is the immediate
result of a blow in the parts about the waistcoat, was
beginning to pass away, and Sheen now felt capable of
taking an interest in sublunary matters once more. His ear
smarted horribly, and when he put up a hand and felt it
the pain was so great that he could barely refrain from
uttering a cry. But, however physically battered he might
be, he was feeling happier and more satisfied with himself
than he had felt for years. He had been beaten, but he had
fought his best, and not given in. Some portion of his self-
respect came back to him as he reviewed the late encounter.

Mr Bevan regarded him approvingly

"He was too heavy for you," he said. "He's a good twelve
stone, I make it. I should put you at ten stone—say ten
stone three. Call it nine stone twelve in condition. But you've
got pluck, sir."

Sheen opened his eyes at this surprising statement.

"Some I've met would have laid down after getting that
first hit, but you got up again. That's the secret of fighting.
Always keep going on. Never give in. You know what
Shakespeare says about the one who first cries, 'Hold,
enough!' Do you read Shakespeare, sir?"

"Yes," said Sheen.

"Ah, now *he* knew his business," said Mr Bevan enthusi-
astically. "*There* was ring-craft, as you may say. *He* wasn't
a novice."

Sheen agreed that Shakespeare had written some good
things in his time.

"That's what you want to remember. Always keep going

on, as the saying is. I was fighting Dick Roberts at the National—an American, he was, from San Francisco. He come at me with his right stretched out, and I think he's going to hit me with it, when blessed if his left don't come out instead, and, my Golly! it nearly knocked a passage through me. Just where that fellow hit you, sir, he hit me. It was just at the end of the round, and I went back to my corner. Jim Blake was seconding me. 'What's this, Jim?' I says, 'is the man mad, or what?' 'Why,' he says, 'he's left-handed, that's what's the matter. Get on top of him.' 'Get on top of him? I says. 'My Golly, I'll get on top of the roof if he's going to hit me another of those.' But I kept on, and got close to him, and he couldn't get in another of them, and he give in after the seventh round."

"What competition was that?" asked Sheen.

Mr Bevan laughed. "It was a twenty-round contest, sir, for seven-fifty aside and the Light Weight Championship of the World."

Sheen looked at him in astonishment. He had always imagined professional pugilists to be bullet-headed and beetle-browed to a man. He was not prepared for one of Mr Joe Bevan's description. For all the marks of his profession that he bore on his face, in the shape of lumps and scars, he might have been a curate. His face looked tough, and his eyes harboured always a curiously alert, questioning expression, as if he were perpetually "sizing up" the person he was addressing. But otherwise he was like other men. He seemed also to have a pretty taste in Literature. This, combined with his strong and capable air, attracted Sheen. Usually he was shy and ill at ease with strangers. Joe Bevan he felt he had known all his life.

"Do you still fight?" he asked.

"No," said Mr Bevan, "I gave it up. A man finds he's getting on, as the saying is, and it don't do to keep at it too long. I teach and I train, but I don't fight now."

A sudden idea flashed across Sheen's mind. He was still glowing with that pride which those who are accustomed to work with their brains feel when they have gone honestly through some labour of the hands. At that moment he felt

himself capable of fighting the world and beating it. The
small point, that Albert had knocked him out of time in less
than a minute, did not damp him at all. He had started on
the right road. He had done something. He had stood up to
his man till he could stand no longer. An unlimited vista of
action stretched before him. He had tasted the pleasure of
the fight, and he wanted more.

Why, he thought, should he not avail himself of Joe
Bevan's services to help him put himself right in the eyes of
the house? At the end of the term, shortly before the Public
Schools' Competitions at Aldershot, inter-house boxing cups
were competed for at Wrykyn. It would be a dramatic act of
reparation to the house if he could win the Light-Weight cup
for it. His imagination, jumping wide gaps, did not admit the
possibility of his not being good enough to win it. In the
scene which he conjured up in his mind he was an easy vic-
tor. After all, there was the greater part of the term to learn
in, and he would have a Champion of the World to teach him.

Mr Bevan cut in on his reflections as if he had heard
them by some process of wireless telegraphy.

"Now, look here, sir," he said, "you should let me give you
a few lessons. You're plucky, but you don't know the game
as yet. And boxing's a thing every one ought to know. Supposition is, you're crossing a field or going down a street
with your sweetheart or your wife—"

Sheen was neither engaged nor married, but he let the
point pass.

—"And up comes one of these hooligans, as they call 'em.
What are you going to do if he starts his games? Why,
nothing, if you can't box. You may be plucky, but you can't
beat him. And if you beat him, you'll get half murdered
yourself. What you want to do is to learn to box, and then
what happens? Why, as soon as he sees you shaping, he
says to himself, 'Hullo, this chap knows too much for me.
I'm off,' and off he runs. Or supposition is, he comes for
you. You don't mind. Not you. You give him one punch in
the right place, and then you go off to your tea, leaving him
lying there. He won't get up."

"I'd like to learn," said Sheen. "I should be awfully

obliged if you'd teach me. I wonder if you could make me any good by the end of the term. The House Competitions come off then."

"That all depends, sir. It comes easier to some than others. If you know how to shoot your left out straight, that's as good as six months' teaching. After that it's all ring-craft. The straight left beats the world."

"Where shall I find you?"

"I'm training a young chap—eight stone seven, and he's got to get down to eight stone four, for a bantam weight match—at an inn up the river here. I daresay you know it, sir. Or any one would tell you where it is. The 'Blue Boar,' it's called. You come there any time you like to name, sir, and you'll find me."

"I should like to come every day," said Sheen. "Would that be too often?"

"Oftener the better, sir. You can't practise too much."

"Then I'll start next week. Thanks very much. By the way, I shall have to go by boat, I suppose. It isn't far, is it? I've not been up the river for some time, The School generally goes down stream."

"It's not what you'd call far," said Bevan. "But it would be easier for you to come by road."

"I haven't a bicycle."

"Wouldn't one of your friends lend you one?"

Sheen flushed.

"No, I'd better come by boat, I think. I'll turn up on Tuesday at about five. Will that suit you?"

"Yes, sir. That will be a good time. Then I'll say good bye, sir, for the present."

Sheen went back to his house in a different mood from the one in which he had left it. He did not care now when the other Seymourites looked through him.

In the passage he met Linton, and grinned pleasantly at him.

"What the dickens was that man grinning at?" said Linton to himself. "I must have a smut or something on my face."

But a close inspection in the dormitory looking-glass revealed no blemish on his handsome features.

VIII

A Naval Battle and Its Consequences

What a go is life!

Let us examine the case of Jackson, of Dexter's. O'Hara, who had left Dexter's at the end of the summer term, had once complained to Clowes of the manner in which his house-master treated him, and Clowes had remarked in his melancholy way that it was nothing less than a breach of the law that Dexter should persist in leading a fellow a dog's life without a dog licence for him.

That was precisely how Jackson felt on the subject.

Things became definitely unbearable on the day after Sheen's interview with Mr Joe Bevan.

'Twas morn—to begin at the beginning—and Jackson sprang from his little cot to embark on the labours of the day. Unfortunately, he sprang ten minutes too late, and came down to breakfast about the time of the second slice of bread and marmalade. Result, a hundred lines. Proceeding to school, he had again fallen foul of his house-master—in whose form he was—over a matter of unprepared Livy. As a matter of fact, Jackson *had* prepared the Livy. Or, rather, he had not absolutely *prepared* it; but he had meant to. But it was Mr Templar's preparation, and Mr Templar was short-sighted. Any one will understand, therefore, that it would have been simply chucking away the gifts of Providence if he had not gone on with the novel which he had been reading up till the last moment before prep-time, and had brought along with him accidentally, as it were. It was a book called *A Spoiler of Men*, by Richard Marsh, and there was a repulsive crime on nearly every page. It was Hot Stuff. Much better than Livy . . .

Lunch Score—Two hundred lines.

During lunch he had the misfortune to upset a glass of

water. Pure accident, of course, but there it *was*, don't you know, all over the table.

Mr Dexter had called him—

(*a*) clumsy;
(*b*) a pig;

and had given him

(1) Advice—"You had better be careful, Jackson".
(2) A present—"Two hundred lines, Jackson".

On the match being resumed at two o'clock, with four hundred lines on the score-sheet, he had played a fine, free game during afternoon school, and Mr Dexter, who objected to fine, free games—or, indeed, any games—during school hours, had increased the total to six hundred, when stumps were drawn for the day.

So on a bright sunny Saturday afternoon, when he should have been out in the field cheering the house-team on to victory against the School House, Jackson sat in the junior day-room at Dexter's copying out portions of Virgil, Æneid Two.

To him, later on in the afternoon, when he had finished half his task, entered Painter, with the news that Dexter's had taken thirty points off the School House just after half-time.

"Mopped them up," said the terse and epigrammatic Painter. "Made rings round them. Haven't you finished yet? Well, chuck it, and come out."

"What's on?" asked Jackson.

"We're going to have a boat race."

"Pile it on."

"We are, really. Fact. Some of these School House kids are awfully sick about the match, and challenged us. That chap Tomlin thinks he can row.

"He can't row for nuts," said Jackson. "He doesn't know which end of the oar to shove into the water. I've seen cats that could row better than Tomlin."

"That's what I told him. At least, I said he couldn't row for toffee, so he said all right, I bet I can lick you, and I said

I betted he couldn't, and he said all right, then, let's try, and then the other chaps wanted to join in, so we made an inter-house thing of it. And I want you to come and stroke us."

Jackson hesitated. Mr Dexter, setting the lines on Friday, had certainly said that they were to be shown up "tomorrow evening." He had said it very loud and clear. Still, in a case like this. . . . After all, by helping to beat the School House on the river he would be giving Dexter's a leg-up. And what more could the man want?

"Right ho," said Jackson.

Down at the School boat-house the enemy were already afloat when Painter and Jackson arrived.

"Buck up," cried the School House crew.

Dexter's embarked, five strong. There was room for two on each seat. Jackson shared the post of stroke with Painter. Crowle steered.

"Ready?" asked Tomlin from the other boat.

"Half a sec.," said Jackson. "What's the course?"

"Oh, don't you know *that* yet? Up to the town, round the island just below the bridge,—the island with the croquet ground on it, *you* know—and back again here. Ready?"

"In a jiffy. Look here, Crowle, remember about steering. You pull the right line if you want to go to the right and the other if you want to go to the left."

"All right," said the injured Crowle. "As if I didn't know that."

"Thought I'd mention it. It's your fault. Nobody could tell by looking at you that you knew anything except how to eat. Ready, you chaps?"

"When I say 'Three,' " said Tomlin.

It was a subject of heated discussion between the crews for weeks afterwards whether Dexter's boat did or did not go off at the word "Two." Opinions were divided on the topic. But it was certain that Jackson and his men led from the start. Pulling a good, splashing stroke which had drenched Crowle to the skin in the first thirty yards, Dexter's boat crept slowly ahead. By the time the island was reached, it led by a length. Encouraged by success, the leaders redoubled their already energetic efforts. Crowle sat in a shower-bath. He was even moved to speech about it.

"When you've finished," said Crowle.

Jackson, intent upon repartee, caught a crab, and the School House drew level again. The two boats passed the island abreast.

Just here occurred one of those unfortunate incidents. Both crews had quickened their stroke until the boats had practically been converted into submarines, and the rival coxswains were observing bitterly to space that this was jolly well the last time they ever let themselves in for this sort of thing, when round the island there hove in sight a flotilla of boats, directly in the path of the racers.

There were three of them, and not even the spray which played over them like a fountain could prevent Crowle from seeing that they were manned by Judies. Even on the river these outcasts wore their mortar-boards.

"Look out!" shrieked Crowle, pulling hard on his right line. "Stop rowing, you chaps. We shall be into them."

At the same moment the School House oarsmen ceased pulling. The two boats came to a halt a few yards from the enemy.

"What's up?" panted Jackson, crimson from his exertions. "Hullo, it's the Judies!"

Tomlin was parleying with the foe.

"Why the dickens can't you keep out of the way? Spoiling our race. Wait till we get ashore."

But the Judies, it seemed, were not prepared to wait even for that short space of time. A miscreant, larger than the common run of Judy, made a brief, but popular, address to his men.

"Splash them!" he said.

Instantly, amid shrieks of approval, oars began to strike the water, and the water began to fly over the Wrykyn boats, which were now surrounded. The latter were not slow to join battle with the same weapons. Homeric laughter came from the bridge above. The town bridge was a sort of loafers' club, to which the entrance fee was a screw of tobacco, and the subscription an occasional remark upon

the weather. Here gathered together day by day that section of the populace which resented it when they "asked for
employment, and only got work instead". From morn till
eve they lounged against the balustrades, surveying nature,
and hoping it would be kind enough to give them some
excitement that day. An occasional dog-fight found in them
an eager audience. No runaway horse ever bored them. A
broken-down motor-car was meat and drink to them. They
had an appetite for every spectacle.

When, therefore, the water began to fly from boat to
boat, kind-hearted men fetched their friends from neigh-
bouring public houses and craned with them over the
parapet, observing the sport and commenting thereon. It
was these comments that attracted Mr Dexter's attention.
When, cycling across the bridge, he found the south side of
it entirely congested, and heard raucous voices urging
certain unseen "little 'uns" now to "go it" and anon to
"vote for Pedder", his curiosity was aroused. He dismounted
and pushed his way through the crowd until he got a clear
view of what was happening below.

He was just in time to see the most stirring incident of
the fight. The biggest of the Judy boats had been propelled
by the current nearer and nearer to the Dexter Argo. No
sooner was it within distance than Jackson, dropping his
oar, grasped the side and pulled it towards him. The two
boats crashed together and rocked violently as the crews
rose from their seats and grappled with one another. A
hurricane of laughter and applause went up from the crowd
upon the bridge.

The next moment both boats were bottom upwards and
drifting sluggishly down towards the island, while the crews
swam like rats for the other boats.

Every Wrykinian had to learn to swim before he was
allowed on the river; so that the peril of Jackson and his
crew was not extreme : and it was soon speedily evident that
swimming was also part of the Judy curriculum, for the
shipwrecked ones were soon climbing drippingly on board
the surviving ships, where they sat and made puddles, and
shrieked defiance at their antagonists.

This was accepted by both sides as the end of the fight, and the combatants parted without further hostilities, each fleet believing that the victory was with them.

And Mr Dexter, mounting his bicycle again, rode home to tell the headmaster.

That evening, after preparation, the headmaster held a reception. Among distinguished visitors were Jackson, Painter, Tomlin, Crowle, and six others.

On the Monday morning the headmaster issued a manifesto to the school after prayers. He had, he said, for some time entertained the idea of placing the town out of bounds. He would do so now. No boy, unless he was a prefect, would be allowed till further notice to cross the town bridge. As regarded the river, for the future boating Wrykinians must confine their attentions to the lower river. Nobody must take a boat up-stream. The school boatman would have strict orders to see that this rule was rigidly enforced. Any breach of these bounds would, he concluded, be punished with the utmost severity.

The headmaster of Wrykyn was not a hasty man. He thought before he put his foot down. But when he did, he put it down heavily.

Sheen heard the ultimatum with dismay. He was a law-abiding person, and here he was, faced with a dilemma that made it necessary for him to choose between breaking school rules of the most important kind, or pulling down all the castles he had built in the air before the mortar had had time to harden between their stones.

He wished he could talk it over with somebody. But he had nobody with whom he could talk over anything. He must think it out for himself.

He spent the rest of the day thinking it out, and by nightfall he had come to his decision.

Even at the expense of breaking bounds and the risk of being caught at it, he must keep his appointment with Joe Bevan. It would mean going to the town landing-stage for a boat, thereby breaking bounds twice over.

But it would have to be done.

IX

SHEEN BEGINS HIS EDUCATION

The "Blue Boar" was a picturesque inn, standing on the bank
of the river Severn. It was much frequented in the summer
by fishermen, who spent their days in punts and their evenings in the old oak parlour, where a picture in boxing
costume of Mr Joe Bevan, whose brother was the landlord
of the inn, gazed austerely down on them, as if he disapproved of the lamentable want of truth displayed by the
majority of their number. Artists also congregated there to
paint the ivy-covered porch. At the back of the house were
bedrooms, to which the fishermen would make their way in
the small hours of a summer morning, arguing to the last as
they stumbled upstairs. One of these bedrooms, larger than
the others, had been converted into a gymnasium for the
use of mine host's brother. Thither he brought pugilistic
aspirants who wished to be trained for various contests, and
it was the boast of the "Blue Boar" that it had never turned
out a loser. A reputation of this kind is a valuable asset to
an inn, and the boxing world thought highly of it, in spite
of the fact that it was off the beaten track. Certainly the
luck of the "Blue Boar" had been surprising.

Sheen pulled steadily up stream on the appointed day,
and after half an hour's work found himself opposite the
little landing-stage at the foot of the inn lawn.

His journey had not been free from adventure. On his
way to the town he had almost run into Mr Templar, and
but for the lucky accident of that gentleman's short sight
must have been discovered. He had reached the landing-
stage in safety, but he had not felt comfortable until he
was well out of sight of the town. It was fortunate for him
in the present case that he was being left so severely alone

by the school. It was an advantage that nobody took the least interest in his goings and comings.

Having moored his boat and proceeded to the inn, he was directed upstairs by the landlord, who was an enlarged and coloured edition of his brother. From the other side of the gymnasium door came an unceasing and mysterious shuffling sound.

He tapped at the door and went in.

He found himself in a large, airy room, lit by two windows and a broad skylight. The floor was covered with linoleum. But it was the furniture that first attracted his attention. In a farther corner of the room was a circular wooden ceiling, supported by four narrow pillars, From the centre of this hung a ball, about the size of an ordinary football. To the left, suspended from a beam, was an enormous leather bolster. On the floor, underneath a table bearing several pairs of boxing-gloves, a skipping-rope, and some wooden dumb-bells, was something that looked like a dozen Association footballs rolled into one. All the rest of the room, a space some few yards square, was bare of furniture. In this space a small sweater-clad youth, with a head of light hair cropped very short, was darting about and ducking and hitting out with both hands at nothing, with such a serious, earnest expression on his face that Sheen could not help smiling. On a chair by one of the windows Mr Joe Bevan was sitting, with a watch in his hand.

As Sheen entered the room the earnest young man made a sudden dash at him. The next moment he seemed to be in a sort of heavy shower of fists. They whizzed past his ear, flashed up from below within an inch of his nose, and tapped him caressingly on the waistcoat. Just as the shower was at its heaviest his assailant darted away again, side-stepped an imaginary blow, ducked another, and came at him once more. None of the blows struck him, but it was with more than a little pleasure that he heard Joe Bevan call "Time!" and saw the active young gentleman sink panting into a seat.

"You and your games, Francis!" said Joe Bevan, reproachfully. "This is a young gentleman from the college come for tuition."

"Gentleman—won't mind—little joke—take it in spirit which is—meant," said Francis, jerkily.

Sheen hastened to assure him that he had not been offended.

"You take your two minutes, Francis," said Mr Bevan, "and then have a turn with the ball. Come this way, Mr—"

"Sheen."

"Come this way, Mr Sheen, and I'll show you where to put on your things."

Sheen had brought his football clothes with him. He had not put them on for a year.

"That's the lad I was speaking of. Getting on prime, he is. Fit to fight for his life, as the saying is."

"What was he doing when I came in?"

"Oh, he always has three rounds like that every day. It teaches you to get about quick. You try it when you get back, Mr. Sheen. Fancy you're fighting me."

"Are you sure I'm not interrupting you in the middle of your work?" asked Sheen.

"Not at all, sir, not at all. I just have to rub him down, and give him his shower-bath, and then he's finished for the day."

Having donned his football clothes and returned to the gymnasium, Sheen found Francis in a chair, having his left leg vigorously rubbed by Mr Bevan.

"You fon' of dargs?" inquired Francis affably, looking up as he came in.

Sheen replied that he was, and, indeed, was possessed of one. The admission stimulated Francis, whose right leg was now under treatment, to a flood of conversation. He, it appeared, had always been one for dargs. Owned two. Answering to the names of Tim and Tom. Beggars for rats, yes. And plucked 'uns? Well—he would like to see, would Francis, a dog that Tim or Tom would not stand up to. Clever, too. Why once—

Joe Bevan cut his soliloquy short at this point by leading him off to another room for his shower-bath; but before he went he expressed a desire to talk further with Sheen on the subject of dogs, and, learning that Sheen would be there every day, said he was glad to hear it. He added that for a brother dog-lover he did not mind stretching a point, so that, if ever Sheen wanted a couple of rounds any day, he, Francis, would see that he got them. This offer, it may be mentioned, Sheen accepted with gratitude, and the extra practice he acquired thereby was subsequently of the utmost use to him. Francis, as a boxer, excelled in what is known in pugilistic circles as shiftiness. That is to say, he had a number of ingenious ways of escaping out of tight corners; and these he taught Sheen, much to the latter's profit.

But this was later, when the Wrykinian had passed those preliminary stages on which he was now to embark.

The art of teaching boxing really well is a gift, and it is given to but a few. It is largely a matter of personal magnetism, and, above all, sympathy. A man may be a fine boxer himself, up to every move of the game, and a champion of champions, but for all that he may not be a good teacher. If he has not the sympathy necessary for the appreciation of the difficulties experienced by the beginner, he cannot produce good results. A boxing instructor needs three qualities —skill, sympathy, and enthusiasm. Joe Bevan had all three, particularly enthusiasm. His heart was in his work, and he carried Sheen with him. "Beautiful, sir, beautiful," he kept saying, as he guarded the blows; and Sheen, though too clever to be wholly deceived by the praise, for he knew perfectly well that his efforts up to the present had been anything but beautiful, was nevertheless encouraged, and put all he knew into his hits. Occasionally Joe Bevan would push out his left glove. Then, if Sheen's guard was in the proper place and the push did not reach its destination, Joe would mutter a word of praise. If Sheen dropped his right hand, so that he failed to stop the blow, Bevan would observe, "Keep that guard up, sir!" with almost a pained intonation, as if he had been disappointed in a friend.

The constant repetition of this maxim gradually drove it into Sheen's head, so that towards the end of the lesson he no longer lowered his right hand when he led with his left; and he felt the gentle pressure of Joe Bevan's glove less frequently. At no stage of a pupil's education did Joe Bevan hit him really hard, and in the first few lessons he could scarcely be said to hit him at all. He merely rested his glove against the pupil's face. On the other hand, he was urgent in imploring the pupil to hit *him* as hard as he could.

"Don't be too kind, sir," he would chant, "*I* don't mind being hit. Let me have it. Don't flap. Put it in with some weight behind it." He was also fond of mentioning that extract from Polonius' speech to Laertes, which he had quoted to Sheen on their first meeting.

Sheen finished his first lesson, feeling hotter than he had ever felt in his life.

"Hullo, sir, you're out of condition," commented Mr Bevan. "Have a bit of a rest."

Once more Sheen had learnt the lesson of his weakness. He could hardly realise that he had only begun to despise himself in the last fortnight. Before then, he had been, on the whole, satisfied with himself. He was brilliant at work, and would certainly get a scholarship at Oxford or Cambridge when the time came; and he had specialised in work to the exclusion of games. It is bad to specialise in games to the exclusion of work, but of the two courses the latter is probably the less injurious. One gains at least health by it.

But Sheen now understood thoroughly, what he ought to have learned from his study of the Classics, that the happy mean was the thing at which to strive. And for the future he meant to aim at it. He would get the Gotford, if he could, but also would he win the house boxing at his weight.

After he had rested he discovered the use of the big ball beneath the table. It was soft, but solid and heavy. By throwing this—the medicine-ball, as they call it in the profession—at Joe Bevan, and catching it, Sheen made himself very hot again, and did the muscles of his shoulders a great deal of good.

"That'll do for today, then, sir." said Joe Bevan. "Have a

good rub down tonight, or you'll find yourself very stiff in the morning."

"Well, do you think I shall be any good?" asked Sheen.

"You'll do fine, sir. But remember what Shakespeare says."

"About vaulting ambition?"

"No, sir, no. I meant what Hamlet says to the players. 'Nor do not saw the air too much, with your hand, thus, but use all gently.' That's what you've got to remember in boxing, sir. Take it easy. Easy and cool does it, and the straight left beats the world."

Sheen paddled quietly back to the town with the stream, pondering over this advice. He felt that he had advanced another step. He was not foolish enough to believe that he knew anything about boxing as yet, but he felt that it would not be long before he did.

X

Sheen's Progress

Sheen improved. He took to boxing as he had taken to fives. He found that his fives helped him. He could get about on his feet quickly, and his eye was trained to rapid work.

His second lesson was not encouraging. He found that he had learned just enough to make him stiff and awkward, and no more. But he kept on, and by the end of the first week Joe Bevan declared definitely that he would do, that he had the root of the matter in him, and now required only practice.

"I wish you could see like I can how you're improving," he said at the end of the sixth lesson, as they were resting after five minutes' exercise with the medicine-ball. "I get four blows in on some of the gentlemen I teach to one what I get in on you. But it's like riding. When you can trot, you look forward to when you can gallop. And when you can gallop, you can't see yourself getting on any further. But you're improving all the time."

"But I can't gallop yet," said Sheen.

"Well, no, not gallop exactly, but you've only had six lessons. Why, in another six weeks, if you come regular, you won't know yourself. You'll be making some of the young gentlemen at the college wish they had never been born. You'll make babies of them, that's what you'll do."

"I'll bet I couldn't, if I'd learnt with some one else," said Sheen, sincerely. "I don't believe I should have learnt a thing if I'd gone to the school instructor."

"Who is your school instructor, sir?"

"A man named Jenkins. He used to be in the army."

"Well, there, you see, that's what it is. I know old George Jenkins. He used to be a pretty good boxer in his time, but there! boxing's a thing, like everything else, that moves with
3—TWF * *

the times. We used to go about in iron trucks. Now we go in motor-cars. Just the same with boxing. What you're learning now is the sort of boxing that wins championship fights nowadays. Old George, well, he teaches you how to put your left out, but, my Golly, he doesn't know any tricks. He hasn't studied it same as I have. It's the ring-craft that wins battles. Now sir, if you're ready."

They put on the gloves again. When the round was over, Mr Bevan had further comments to make.

"You don't hit hard enough, sir," he said. "Don't flap. Let it come straight out with some weight behind it. You want to be earnest in the ring. The other man's going to do his best to hurt you, and you've got to stop him. One good punch is worth twenty taps. You hit him. And when you've hit him, don't you go back; you hit him again. They'll only give you three rounds in any competition you go in for, so you want to do the work you can while you're at it."

As the days went by, Sheen began to imbibe some of Joe Bevan's rugged philosophy of life. He began to understand that the world is a place where every man has to look after himself, and that it is the stronger hand that wins. That sentence from *Hamlet* which Joe Bevan was so fond of quoting practically summed up the whole duty of man—and boy too. One should not seek quarrels, but, "being in," one should do one's best to ensure that one's opponent thought twice in future before seeking them. These afternoons at the "Blue Boar" were gradually giving Sheen what he had never before possessed—self-confidence. He was beginning to find that he was capable of something after all, that in an emergency he would be able to keep his end up. The feeling added a zest to all that he did. His work in school improved. He looked at the Gotford no longer as a prize which he would have to struggle to win. He felt that his rivals would have to struggle to win it from him.

After his twelfth lesson, when he had learned the ground-work of the art, and had begun to develop a style of his own, like some nervous batsman at cricket who does not show his true form till he has been at the wickets for several overs, the dog-loving Francis gave him a trial. This was a

very different affair from his spars with Joe Bevan. Frank
Hunt was one of the cleverest boxers at his weight in England, but he had not Joe Bevan's gift of hitting gently. He
probably imagined that he was merely tapping, and certainly his blows were not to be compared with those he
delivered in the exercise of his professional duties; but,
nevertheless, Sheen had never felt anything so painful before, not even in his passage of arms with Albert. He came
out of the encounter with a swollen lip and a feeling that
one of his ribs was broken, and he had not had the pleasure
of landing a single blow upon his slippery antagonist, who
flowed about the room like quicksilver. But he had not
flinched, and the statement of Francis, as they shook hands,
that he had "done varry well," was as balm. Boxing is one
of the few sports where the loser can feel the same thrill of
triumph as the winner. There is no satisfaction equal to that
which comes when one has forced oneself to go through an
ordeal from which one would have liked to have escaped.

"Capital, sir, capital," said Joe Bevan. "I wanted to see
whether you would lay down or not when you began to get
a few punches. You did capitally, Mr Sheen."

"I didn't hit him much," said Sheen with a laugh.

"Never mind, sir, you got hit, which was just as good.
Some of the gentlemen I've taught wouldn't have taken half
that. They're all right when they're on top and winning, and
to see them shape you'd say to yourself, By George, here's a
champion. But let 'em get a punch or two, and hullo! says
you, what's this? They don't like it. They lay down. But you
kept on. There's one thing, though, you want to keep that
guard up when you duck. You slip him that way once. Very
well. Next time he's waiting for you. He doesn't hit straight.
He hooks you, and you don't want many of those."

Sheen enjoyed his surreptitious visits to the "Blue Boar."
Twice he escaped being caught in the most sensational way;
and once Mr Spence, who looked after the Wrykyn cricket
and gymnasium, and played everything equally well, nearly
caused complications by inviting Sheen to play fives with
him after school. Fortunately the Gotford afforded an
excellent excuse. As the time for the examination drew near,

those who had entered for it were accustomed to become hermits to a great extent, and to retire after school to work in their studies.

"You mustn't overdo it, Sheen," said Mr Spence. "You ought to get some exercise."

"Oh, I do, sir," said Sheen. "I still play fives, but I play before breakfast now."

He had had one or two games with Harrington of the School House, who did not care particularly whom he played with so long as his opponent was a useful man. Sheen being one of the few players in the school who were up to his form, Harrington ignored the cloud under which Sheen rested. When they met in the world outside the fives-courts Harrington was polite, but made no overtures of friendship. That, it may be mentioned, was the attitude of every one who did not actually cut Sheen. The exception was Jack Bruce, who had constituted himself audience to Sheen, when the latter was practising the piano, on two further occasions. But then Bruce was so silent by nature that for all practical purposes he might just as well have cut Sheen like the others.

"We might have a game before breakfast some time, then," said Mr Spence.

He had noticed, being a master who did notice things, that Sheen appeared to have few friends, and had made up his mind that he would try and bring him out a little. Of the real facts of the case, he knew of course, nothing.

"I should like to, sir," said Sheen.

"Next Wednesday?"

"All right, sir."

"I'll be there at seven. If you're before me, you might get the second court, will you?"

The second court from the end nearest the boarding-house was the best of the half-dozen fives-courts at Wrykyn. After school sometimes you would see fags racing across the gravel to appropriate it for their masters. The rule was that whoever first pinned to the door a piece of paper with his name on it was the legal owner of the court—and it was a stirring sight to see a dozen fags fighting to get at the door.

But before breakfast the court might be had with less trouble.

Meanwhile, Sheen paid his daily visits to the "Blue Boar," losing flesh and gaining toughness with every lesson. The more he saw of Joe Bevan the more he liked him, and appreciated his strong, simple outlook on life. Shakespeare was a great bond between them. Sheen had always been a student of the Bard, and he and Joe would sit on the little verandah of the inn, looking over the river, until it was time for him to row back to the town, quoting passages at one another. Joe Bevan's knowledge of the plays, especially the tragedies, was wide, and at first inexplicable to Sheen. It was strange to hear him declaiming long speeches from *Macbeth* or *Hamlet*, and to think that he was by profession a pugilist. One evening he explained his curious erudition. In his youth, before he took to the ring in earnest, he had travelled with a Shakespearean repertory company. "I never played a star part," he confessed, "but I used to come on in the Battle of Bosworth and in Macbeth's castle and what not. I've been First Citizen sometimes. I was the carpenter in *Julius Cæsar*. That was my biggest part. 'Truly sir, in respect of a fine workman, I am but, as you would say, a cobbler.' But somehow the stage—well . . . *you* know what it is, sir. Leeds one week, Manchester the next, Brighton the week after, and travelling all Sunday. It wasn't quiet enough for me."

The idea of becoming a professional pugilist for the sake of peace and quiet tickled Sheen. "But I've always read Shakespeare ever since then," continued Mr Bevan, "and I always shall read him."

It was on the next day that Mr Bevan made a suggestion which drew confidences from Sheen, in his turn.

"What you want now, sir," he said, "is to practise on someone of about your own form, as the saying is. Isn't there some gentleman friend of yours at the college who would come here with you?"

They were sitting on the verandah when he asked this question. It was growing dusk, and the evening seemed to invite confidences. Sheen, looking out across the river and avoiding his friend's glance, explained just what it was that made it so difficult for him to produce a gentleman friend at that particular time. He could feel Mr Bevan's eye upon him, but he went through with it till the thing was told—boldly, and with no attempt to smooth over any of the unpleasant points.

"Never you mind, sir," said Mr Bevan consolingly, as he finished. "We all lose our heads sometimes. I've seen the way you stand up to Francis, and I'll eat—I'll eat the medicine-ball if you're not as plucky as anyone. It's simply a question of keeping your head. You wouldn't do a thing like that again, not you. Don't you worry yourself, sir. We're all alike when we get bustled. We don't know what we're doing, and by the time we've put our hands up and got into shape, why, it's all over, and there you are. Don't you worry yourself, sir."

"You're an awfully good sort, Joe," said Sheen gratefully.

XI

A SMALL INCIDENT

Failing a gentleman friend, Mr Bevan was obliged to do what he could by means of local talent. On Sheen's next visit he was introduced to a burly youth of his own age, very taciturn, and apparently ferocious. He, it seemed, was the knife and boot boy at the "Blue Boar", "did a bit" with the gloves, and was willing to spar with Sheen provided Mr Bevan made it all right with the guv'nor; saw, that is so say, that he did not get into trouble for passing in unprofessional frivolity moments which should have been sacred to knives and boots. These terms having been agreed to, he put on the gloves.

For the first time since he had begun his lessons, Sheen experienced an attack of his old shyness and dislike of hurting other people's feelings. He could not resist the thought that he had no grudge against the warden of the knives and boots. He hardly liked to hit him.

The other, however, did not share this prejudice. He rushed at Sheen with such determination, that almost the first warning the latter had that the contest had begun was the collision of the back of his head with the wall. Out in the middle of the room he did better, and was beginning to hold his own, in spite of a rousing thump on his left eye, when Joe Bevan called "Time!" A second round went off in much the same way. His guard was more often in the right place, and his leads less wild. At the conclusion of the round, pressure of business forced his opponent to depart, and Sheen wound up his lesson with a couple of minutes at the punching-ball. On the whole, he was pleased with his first spar with someone who was really doing his best and trying to hurt him. With Joe Bevan and Francis there was always the feeling that they were playing down to him. Joe Bevan's gentle taps, in particular, were a little humiliating. But with his late opponent all had been serious. It had been a real test, and he had come through it very fairly. On the whole, he had taken more than he had given —his eye would look curious tomorrow—but already he had thought out a way of foiling the burly youth's rushes. Next time he would really show his true form.

The morrow, on which Sheen expected his eye to look curious, was the day he had promised to play fives with Mr Spence. He hoped that at the early hour at which they had arranged to play it would not have reached its worst stage; but when he looked in the glass at a quarter to seven, he beheld a small ridge of purple beneath it. It was not large, nor did it interfere with his sight, but it was very visible. Mr Spence, however, was a sportsman, and had boxed himself in his time, so there was a chance that nothing would be said.

It was a raw, drizzly morning. There would probably be few fives-players before breakfast, and the capture of the second court should be easy. So it turned out. Nobody was about when Sheen arrived. He pinned his slip of paper to the door, and, after waiting for a short while for Mr Spence and finding the process chilly, went for a trot round the gymnasium to pass the time.

Mr Spence had not arrived during his absence, but somebody else had. At the door of the second court, gleaming in first-fifteen blazer, sweater, stockings, and honour-cap, stood Attell.

Sheen looked at Attell, and Attell looked through Sheen.

It was curious, thought Sheen, that Attell should be standing in the very doorway of court two. It seemed to suggest that he claimed some sort of ownership. On the other hand, there was his, Sheen's, paper on the . . . His eye happened to light on the cement flooring in front of the court. There was a crumpled ball of paper there.

When he had started for his run, there had been no such ball of paper.

Sheen picked it up and straightened it out. On it was written "R. D. Sheen".

He looked up quickly. In addition to the far-away look, Attell's face now wore a faint smile, as if he had seen something rather funny on the horizon. But he spake no word.

A curiously calm and contented feeling came upon Sheen. Here was something definite at last. He could do nothing, however much he might resent it, when fellows passed him by as if he did not exist; but when it came to removing his landmark . . .

"Would you mind shifting a bit?" he said very politely. "I want to pin my paper on the door again. It seems to have fallen down."

Attell's gaze shifted slowly from the horizon and gradually embraced Sheen.

"I've got this court," he said.

"I think not," said Sheen silkily. "I was here at ten to seven, and there was no paper on the door then. So I put mine up. If you move a little, I'll put it up again."

"Go and find another court, if you want to play," said Attell, "and if you've got anybody to play with," he added with a sneer. "This is mine."

"I think not," said Sheen.

Attell resumed his inspection of the horizon.

"Attell," said Sheen.

Attell did not answer.

Sheen pushed him gently out of the way, and tore down the paper from the door.

Their eyes met. Attell, after a moment's pause, came forward, half-menacing, half irresolute; and as he came Sheen hit him under the chin in the manner recommended by Mr Bevan.

"When you upper-cut," Mr Bevan was wont to say, "don't make it a swing. Just a half-arm jolt's all you want."

It was certainly all Attell wanted. He was more than surprised. He was petrified. The sudden shock of the blow, coming as it did from so unexpected a quarter, deprived him of speech : which was, perhaps, fortunate for him, for what he would have said would hardly have commended itself to Mr Spence, who came up at this moment.

"Well, Sheen," said Mr Spence, "here you are. I hope

I haven't kept you waiting. What a morning! You've got the court, I hope?"

"Yes, sir," said Sheen.

He wondered if the master had seen the little episode which had taken place immediately before his arrival. Then he remembered that it had happened inside the court. It must have been over by the time Mr Spence had come upon the scene.

"Are you waiting for somebody, Attell?" asked Mr Spence. "Stanning? He will be here directly. I passed him on the way."

Attell left the court, and they began their game.

"You've hurt your eye, Sheen," said Mr Spence, at the end of the first game. "How did that happen?"

"Boxing, sir," said Sheen.

"Oh," replied Mr Spence, and to Sheen's relief he did not pursue his inquiries.

Attell had wandered out across the gravel to meet Stanning.

"Got that court?" inquired Stanning.

"No."

"You idiot, why on earth didn't you? It's the only court worth playing in. Who's got it?"

"Sheen."

"Sheen !"Stanning stopped dead. "Do you mean to say you let a fool like Sheen take it from you ! Why didn't you turn him out?"

"I couldn't," said Attell. "I was just going to when Spence came up. He's playing Sheen this morning. I couldn't very well bag the court when a master wanted it."

"I suppose not," said Stanning. "What did Sheen say when you told him you wanted the court?"

This was getting near a phase of the subject which Attell was not eager to discuss.

"Oh, he didn't say much," he said.

"Did you do anything?" persisted Stanning.

Attell suddenly remembered having noticed that Sheen was wearing a black eye. This was obviously a thing to be turned to account.

"I hit him in the eye," he said. "I'll bet it's coloured by school-time."

And sure enough, when school-time arrived, there was Sheen with his face in the condition described, and Stanning hastened to spread abroad this sequel to the story of Sheen's failings in the town battle. By the end of preparation it had got about the school that Sheen had cheeked Attell, that Attell had hit Sheen, and that Sheen had been afraid to hit him back. At the precise moment when Sheen was in the middle of a warm two-minute round with Francis at the "Blue Boar," an indignation meeting was being held in the senior day-room at Seymour's to discuss this latest disgrace to the house.

"This is getting a bit too thick," was the general opinion. Moreover, it was universally agreed that something ought to be done. The feeling in the house against Sheen had been stirred to a dangerous pitch by this last episode. Seymour's thought more of their reputation than any house in the school. For years past the house had led on the cricket and football field and off it. Sometimes other houses would actually win one of the cups, but, when this happened, Seymour's was always their most dangerous rival. Other houses had their ups and downs, were very good one year and very bad the next; but Seymour's had always managed to maintain a steady level of excellence. It always had a man or two in the School eleven and fifteen, generally supplied one of the School Racquets pair for Queen's Club in the Easter vac., and when this did not happen always had one of two of the Gym. Six or Shooting Eight, or a few men who had won scholarships at the 'Varsities. The pride of a house is almost keener than the pride of a school. From the first minute he entered the house a new boy was made to feel that, in coming to Seymour's, he had accepted a responsibility that his reputation was not his own, but belonged to the house. If he did well, the glory would be Seymour's glory. If he did badly, he would be sinning against the house.

This second story about Sheen, therefore, stirred Seymour's to the extent of giving the house a resemblance to a hornet's nest into which a stone had been hurled. After school that day the house literally hummed. The noise of the two day-rooms talking it over could be heard in the road outside. The only bar that stood between the outraged Seymourites and Sheen was Drummond. As had happened before, Drummond resolutely refused to allow anything in the shape of an active protest, and no argument would draw him from this unreasonable attitude, though why it was that he had taken it up he himself could not have said. Perhaps it was that rooted hatred a boxer instinctively acquires of anything in the shape of unfair play that influenced him. He revolted against the idea of a whole house banding together against one of its members.

So even this fresh provocation did not result in any active interference with Sheen; but it was decided that he must be cut even more thoroughly than before.

And about the time when this was resolved, Sheen was receiving the congratulations of Francis on having positively landed a blow upon him. It was an event which marked an epoch in his career.

XII

DUNSTABLE AND LINTON GO UP THE RIVER

There are some proud, spirited natures which resent rules and laws on principle as attempts to interfere with the rights of the citizen. As the Duchess in the play said of her son, who had had unpleasantness with the authorities at Eton because they had been trying to teach him things, "Silwood is a sweet boy, but he will not stand the bearing-rein". Dunstable was also a sweet boy, but he, too, objected to the bearing-rein. And Linton was a sweet boy, and he had similar prejudices. And this placing of the town out of bounds struck both of them simultaneously as a distinct attempt on the part of the headmaster to apply the bearing-rein.

"It's all very well to put it out of bounds for the kids," said Dunstable, firmly, "but when it comes to Us—why, I never heard of such a thing."

Linton gave it as his opinion that such conduct was quite in a class of its own as regarded cool cheek.

"It fairly sneaks," said Linton, with forced calm, "the Garibaldi."

"Kids," proceeded Dunstable, judicially, "are idiots, and can't be expected to behave themselves down town. Put the show out of bounds to them if you like. But We—"

"We!" echoed Linton.

"The fact is," said Dunstable, "it's a beastly nuisance, but we shall have to go down town and up the river just to assert ourselves. We can't have the thin end of the wedge coming and spoiling our liberties. We may as well chuck life altogether if we aren't able to go to the town whenever we like."

"And Albert will be pining away," added Linton.

"Hullo, young gentlemen," said the town boatman, when they presented themselves to him, "what can I do for you?"

"I know it seems strange," said Dunstable, "but we want a boat. We are the Down-trodden British Schoolboys' League for Demanding Liberty and seeing that We Get It. Have you a boat?"

The man said he believed he had a boat. In fact, now that he came to think of it, he rather fancied he had one or two. He proceeded to get one ready, and the two martyrs to the cause stepped in.

Dunstable settled himself in the stern, and collected the rudder-lines.

"Hullo," said Linton, "aren't you going to row?"

"It may be only my foolish fancy," replied Dunstable, "but I rather think you're going to do that. I'll steer."

"Beastly slacker," said Linton. "Anyhow, how far are we going? I'm not going to pull all night."

"If you row for about half an hour without exerting yourself—and I can trust you not to do that—and then look to your left, you'll see a certain hostelry, if it hasn't moved since I was last there. It's called the 'Blue Boar'. We will have tea there, and then I'll pull gently back, and that will end the programme."

"Except being caught in the town by half the masters," said Linton. "Still, I'm not grumbling. This had to be done. Ready?"

"Not just yet," said Dunstable, looking past Linton and up the landing-stage. "Wait just one second. Here are some friends of ours."

Linton looked over his shoulder.

"Albert!" he cried.

"And the blighter in the bowler who struck me divers blows in sundry places. Ah, they've sighted us."

"What are you going to do?" We can't have another scrap with them."

"Far from it," said Dunstable gently. "Hullo, Albert.

And my friend in the moth-eaten bowler! This is well met."

"You come out here," said Albert, pausing on the brink.

"Why?" asked Dunstable.

"You see what you'll get."

"But we don't want to see what we'll get. You've got such a narrow mind, Albert—may I call you Bertie? You seem to think that nobody has any pleasures except vulgar brawls. We are going to row up river, and think beautiful thoughts."

Albert was measuring with his eye the distance between the boat and landing-stage. It was not far. A sudden spring. . . .

"If you want a fight, go up to the school and ask for Mr Drummond. He's the gentlemen who sent you to hospital last time. Any time you're passing, I'm sure he'd—"

Albert leaped.

But Linton had had him under observation, and, as he sprung, pushed vigorously with his oar. The gap between boat and shore widened in an instant, and Albert, failing to obtain a foothold on the boat, fell back, with a splash that sent a cascade over his friend and the boatman, into three feet of muddy water. By the time he had scrambled out, his enemies were moving pensively up-stream.

The boatman was annoyed.

"Makin' me wet and spoilin' my paint—what yer mean by it?"

"Me and my friend here we want a boat," said Albert, ignoring the main issue.

"Want a boat! Then you'll not get a boat. Spoil my cushions, too, would you? What next, I wonder! You go to Smith and ask *him* for a boat. Perhaps he ain't so particular about having his cushions—"

"Orl right," said Albert, "*orl* right."

Mr Smith proved more complaisant, and a quarter of an hour after Dunstable and Linton had disappeared, Albert and his friend were on the water. Moist outside, Albert burned with a desire for Revenge. He meant to follow his men till he found them. It almost seemed as if there would be a repetition of the naval battle which had caused the town to be put out of bounds. Albert was a quick-tempered youth, and he had swallowed fully a pint of Severn water.

Dunstable and Linton sat for some time in the oak parlour of the "Blue Boar". It was late when they went out. As they reached the water's edge Linton uttered a cry of consternation.

"What's up?" asked Dunstable. "I wish you wouldn't do that so suddenly. It gives me a start. Do you feel bad?"

"Great Scott! it's gone."

"The pain?"

"Our boat. I tied it up to this post."

"You can't have done. What's that boat over there! That looks like ours."

"No, it isn't. That was there when we came. I noticed it. I tied ours up here, to this post."

"This is a shade awkward," said Dunstable thoughfully. "You must have tied it up jolly rottenly. It must have slipped away and gone down-stream. This is where we find ourselves in the cart. Right among the ribstons, by Jove. I feel like that Frenchman in the story, who lost his glasses just as he got to the top of the mountain, and missed the view. Altogezzer I do not vish I 'ad kom."

"I'm certain I tied it up all right. And—why, look! here's the rope still on the pole, just as I left it."

For the first time Dunstable seemed interested.

"This is getting mysterious. Did we hire a rowing-boat or a submarine? There's something on the end of this rope. Give it a tug, and see. There, didn't you feel it?"

"I do believe," said Linton in an awed voice, "the thing's sunk."

They pulled at the rope together. The waters heaved and broke, and up came the nose of the boat, to sink back with a splash as they loosened their hold.

"There are more things in Heaven and Earth—" said Dunstable, wiping his hands. "If you ask me, I should say an enemy hath done this. A boat doesn't sink of its own accord."

"Albert!" said Linton. "The blackguard must have followed us up and done it while we were at tea."

"That's about it," said Dunstable. "And now—how about getting home?"

"I suppose we'd better walk. We shall be hours late for lock-up."

"You," said Dunstable, "may walk if you are fond of exercise and aren't in a hurry. Personally, I'm going back by river."

"But—"

"That looks a good enough boat over there. Anyhow, we must make it do. One mustn't be particular for once."

"But it belongs—what will the other fellow do?"

"I can't help *his* troubles," said Dunstable mildly, "having enough of my own. Coming?"

It was about ten minutes later that Sheen, approaching the waterside in quest of his boat, found no boat there. The time was a quarter to six, and lock-up was at six-thirty.

XIII

Deus Ex Machina

It did not occur to Sheen immediately that his boat had actually gone. The full beauty of the situation was some moments in coming home to him. At first he merely thought that somebody had moved it to another part of the bank, as the authorities at the inn had done once or twice in the past, to make room for the boats of fresh visitors. Walking along the lawn in search of it, he came upon the stake to which Dunstable's submerged craft was attached. He gave the rope a tentative pull, and was surprised to find that there was a heavy drag on the end of it.

Then suddenly the truth flashed across him. "Heavens!" he cried, "it's sunk."

Joe Bevan and other allies lent their aid to the pulling. The lost boat came out of the river like some huge fish, and finally rested on the bank, oozing water and drenching the grass in all directions.

Joe Bevan stooped down, and examined it in the dim light.

"What's happened here, sir," he said, "is that there's a plank gone from the bottom. Smashed clean out, it is. Not started it isn't. Smashed clean out. That's what it is. Some one must have been here and done it."

Sheen looked at the boat, and saw that he was right. A plank in the middle had been splintered. It looked as if somebody had driven some heavy instrument into it. As a matter of fact, Albert had effected the job with the butt-end of an oar.

The damage was not ruinous. A carpenter could put the thing right at no great expense. But it would take time. And meanwhile the minutes were flying, and lock-up was now little more than half an hour away.

"What'll you do, sir?" asked Bevan.

That was just what Sheen was asking himself. What could he do? The road to the school twisted and turned to such an extent that, though the distance from the "Blue Boar" to Seymour's was only a couple of miles as the crow flies, he would have to cover double that distance unless he took a short cut across the fields. And if he took a short cut in the dark he was certain to lose himself. It was a choice of evils. The "Blue Boar" possessed but one horse and trap, and he had seen that driven away to the station in charge of a fisherman's luggage half an hour before.

"I shall have to walk," he said.

"It's a long way. You'll be late, won't you?" said Mr Bevan.

"It can't be helped. I suppose I shall. I wonder who smashed that boat," he added after a pause.

Passing through the inn on his way to the road, he made inquiries. It appeared that two young gentlemen from the school had been there to tea. They had arrived in a boat and gone away in a boat. Nobody else had come into the inn. Suspicion obviously rested upon them.

"Do you remember anything about them?" asked Sheen.

Further details came out. One of the pair had worn a cap like Sheen's. The other's headgear, minutely described, showed him that its owner was a member of the school second eleven.

Sheen pursued the inquiry. He would be so late in any case that a minute or so more or less would make no material difference; and he was very anxious to find out, if possible, who it was that had placed him in this difficulty. He knew that he was unpopular in the school, but he had not looked for this sort of thing.

Then somebody suddenly remembered having heard one of the pair address the other by name.

"What name?" asked Sheen.

His informant was not sure. Would it be Lindon?

"Linton," said Sheen.

That was it.

Sheen thanked him and departed, still puzzled. Linton, as

he knew him, was not the sort of fellow to do a thing like that. And the other, the second eleven man, must be Dunstable. They were always about together. He did not know much about Dunstable, but he could hardly believe that this sort of thing was his form either. Well, he would have to think of that later. He must concentrate himself now on covering the distance to the school in the minimum of time. He looked at his watch. Twenty minutes more. If he hurried, he might not be so very late. He wished that somebody would come by in a cart, and give him a lift.

He stopped and listened. No sound of horse's hoof broke the silence. He walked on again.

Then, faint at first, but growing stronger every instant, there came from some point in the road far behind him a steady droning sound. He almost shouted with joy. A motor! Even now he might do it.

But could he stop it? Would the motorist pay any attention to him, or would he flash past and leave him in the dust? From the rate at which the drone increased the car seemed to be travelling at a rare speed.

He moved to one side of the road, and waited. He could see the lights now, flying towards him.

Then, as the car hummed past, he recognised its driver, and put all he knew into a shout.

"Bruce!" he cried.

For a moment it seemed as if he had not been heard. The driver paid not the smallest attention, as far as he could see. He looked neither to the left nor to right. Then the car slowed down, and, backing, came slowly to where he stood.

"Hullo," said the driver, "who's that?"

Jack Bruce was alone in the car, muffled to the eyes in an overcoat. It was more by his general appearance than his face that Sheen had recognised him.

"It's me, Sheen. I say, Bruce, I wish you'd give me a lift to Seymour's, will you?"

There was never any waste of words about Jack Bruce. Of all the six hundred and thirty-four boys at Wrykyn he was probably the only one whose next remark in such cir-

cumstances would not have been a question. Bruce seldom
asked questions—never, if they wasted time.

"Hop in," he said.

Sheen consulted his watch again.

"Lock-up's in a quarter of an hour," he said, "but they
give us ten minutes' grace. That allows us plenty of time,
doesn't it?"

"Do it in seven minutes, if you like."

"Don't hurry," said Sheen. "I've never been in a motor
before, and I don't want to cut the experience short. It's
awfully good of you to give me a lift."

"That's all right," said Bruce.

"Were you going anywhere? Am I taking you out of your
way?"

"No. I was just trying the car. It's a new one. The pater's
just got it."

"Do you do much of this?" said Sheen.

"Good bit. I'm going in for the motor business when I
leave school."

"So all this is training?"

"That's it."

There was a pause.

"You seemed to be going at a good pace just now," said
Sheen.

"About thirty miles an hour. She can move all right."

"That's faster than you're allowed to go, isn't it?"

"Yes."

"You've never been caught, have you?"

"Not yet. I want to see how much pace I can get out of
her, because she'll be useful when the election really comes
on. Bringing voters to the poll, you know. That's why the
pater bought this new car. It's a beauty. His other's only
a little runabout."

"Doesn't your father mind your motoring?"

"Likes it," said Jack Bruce.

It seemed to Sheen that it was about time that he volunteered some information about himself, instead of plying his
companion with questions. It was pleasant talking to a
Wrykinian again; and Jack Bruce had apparently either not

heard of the Albert incident, or else he was not influenced by it in any way.

"You've got me out of an awful hole, Bruce," he began.

"That's all right. Been out for a walk?"

"I'd been to the 'Blue Boar'. "

"Oh!" said Bruce. He did not seem to wish to know why Sheen had been there.

Sheen proceeded to explain.

"I suppose you've heard all about me," he said uncomfortably. "About the town, you know. That fight. Not joining in."

"Heard something about it," said Bruce.

"I went down town again after that," said Sheen, "and met the same fellows who were fighting Linton and the others. They came for me, and I was getting awfully mauled when Joe Bevan turned up."

"Oh, is Joe back again?"

"Do you know him?" asked Sheen in surprise.

"Oh yes. I used to go to the 'Blue Boar' to learn boxing from him all last summer holidays."

"Did you really? Why, that's what I'm doing now."

"Good man," said Bruce.

"Isn't he a splendid teacher?"

"Ripping."

"But I didnt know you boxed, Bruce. You never went in for any of the School competitions."

"I'm rather a rotten weight. Ten six. Too heavy for the Light-Weights and not heavy enough for the Middles. Besides, the competitions here are really inter-house. They don't want day-boys going in for them. Are you going to box for Seymour's?"

"That's what I want to do. You see, it would be rather a score, wouldn't it? After what's happened, you know."

"I suppose it would."

"I should like to do something. It's not very pleasant," he added, with a forced laugh, "being considered a disgrace to the house, and cut by everyone."

"Suppose not."

"The difficulty is Drummond. You see, we are both the

same weight, and he's much better than I am. I'm hoping that he'll go in for the Middles and let me take the Light-Weights. There's nobody he couldn't beat in the Middles, though he would be giving away a stone."

"Have you asked him?"

"Not yet. I want to keep it dark that I'm learning to box, just at present."

"Spring it on them suddenly?"

"Yes. Of course, I can't let it get about that I go to Joe Bevan, because I have to break bounds every time I do it."

"The upper river's out of bounds now for boarders, isn't it?"

"Yes."

Jack Bruce sat in silence for a while, his gaze concentrated on the road in front of him.

"Why go by river at all?" he said at last. "If you like, I'll run you to the 'Blue Boar' in the motor every day."

"Oh, I say, that's awfully decent of you," said Sheen.

"I should like to see old Joe again. I think I'll come and spar, too. If you're learning, what you want more than anything is somebody your own size to box with."

"That's just what Joe was saying. Will you really? I should be awfully glad if you would. Boxing with Joe is all right, but you feel all the time he's fooling with you. I should like to try how I got on with somebody else."

"You'd better meet me here, then, as soon after school as you can."

As he spoke, the car stopped.

"Where are we?" asked Sheen.

"Just at the corner of the road behind the houses."

"Oh, I know. Hullo, there goes the lock-up bell. I shall do it comfortably."

He jumped down.

"I say, Bruce," he said, "I really am most awfully obliged for the lift. Something went wrong with my boat, and I couldn't get back in it. I should have been frightfully in the cart if you hadn't come by."

"That's all right," said Jack Bruce. "I say, Sheen!"

"Hullo?"

"Are you going to practise in the music-room after morning school tomorrow?"

"Yes. Why?"

"I think I'll turn up."

"I wish you would."

"What's that thing that goes like this? I forget most of it.
He whistled a few bars.

"That's a thing of Greig's," said Sheen.

"You might play it tomorrow," said Bruce.

"Rather. Of course I will."

"Thanks," said Jack Bruce. "Good night."

He turned the car, and vanished down the road. From the sound Sheen judged that he was once more travelling at a higher rate of speed than the local police would have approved.

XIV

A Skirmish

Upon consideration Sheen determined to see Linton about that small matter of the boat without delay. After prayers that night he went to his study.

"Can I speak to you for a minute, Linton?" he said.

Linton was surprised. He disapproved of this intrusion. When a fellow is being cut by the house, he ought, by all the laws of school etiquette, to behave as such, and not speak till he is spoken to.

"What do you want?" asked Linton.

"I shan't keep you long. Do you think you could put away that book for a minute, and listen?"

Linton hesitated, then shut the book.

"Hurry up, then," he said.

"I was going to," said Sheen. "I simply came in to tell you that I know perfectly well who sunk my boat this afternoon."

He felt at once that he had now got Linton's undivided attention.

"Your boat!" said Linton. "You don't mean to say that was yours! What on earth were you doing at the place?"

"I don't think that's any business of yours, is it, Linton?"

"How did you get back?"

"I don't think that's any business of yours, either. I daresay you're disappointed, but I did manage to get back. In time for lock-up, too."

"But I don't understand. Do you mean to say that that was your boat we took?"

"Sunk," corrected Sheen.

"Don't be a fool, Sheen. What the dickens should we want to sink your boat for? What happened was this. Albert

—you remember Albert?—followed us up to the inn, and smashed our boat while we were having tea. When we got out and found it sunk, we bagged the only other one we could see. We hadn't a notion it was yours. We thought it belonged to some fisherman chap."

"Then you didn't sink my boat?"

"Of course we didn't. What do you take us for?"

"Sorry," said Sheen. "I thought it was a queer thing for you to have done. I'm glad it wasn't you. Good night."

"But look here," said Linton, "don't go. It must have landed you in a frightful hole, didn't it?"

"A little. But it doesn't matter. Good night."

"But half a second, Sheen—"

Sheen had disappeared.

Linton sat on till lights were turned off, ruminating. He had a very tender conscience where other members of the school were concerned, though it was tougher as regarded masters; and he was full of remorse at the thought of how nearly he had got Sheen into trouble by borrowing his boat that afternoon. It seemed to him that it was his duty to make it up to him in some way.

It was characteristic of Linton that the episode did not, in any way, alter his attitude towards Sheen. Another boy in a similar position might have become effusively friendly. Linton looked on the affair in a calm, judicial spirit. He had done Sheen a bad turn, but that was no reason why he should fling himself on his neck and swear eternal friendship. His demeanour on the occasions when they came in contact with each other remained the same. He did not speak to him, and he did not seem to see him. But all the while he was remembering that somehow or other he must do him a good turn of some sort, by way of levelling things up again. When that good turn had been done, he might dismiss him from his thoughts altogether.

Sheen, for his part, made no attempt to trade on the matter of the boat. He seemed as little anxious to be friendly with Linton as Linton was to be friendly with him. For this Linton was grateful, and continued to keep his eyes open in the hope of finding some opportunity of squaring up matters between them.

His chance was not long in coming. The feeling in the house against Sheen, caused by the story of his encounter with Attell, had not diminished. Stanning had fostered it in various little ways. It was not difficult. When a house of the standing in the school which Seymour's possessed exhibits a weak spot, the rest of the school do not require a great deal of encouragement to go on prodding that weak spot. In short, the school rotted Seymour's about Sheen, and Seymour's raged impotently. Fags of other houses expended much crude satire on Seymour's fags, and even the seniors of the house came in for their share of the baiting. Most of the houses at Wrykyn were jealous of Seymour's, and this struck them as an admirable opportunity of getting something of their own back.

One afternoon, not long after Sheen's conversation with Linton, Stanning came into Seymour's senior day-room and sat down on the table. The senior day-room objected to members of other houses coming and sitting on their table as if they had bought that rickety piece of furniture; but Stanning's reputation as a bruiser kept their resentment within bounds.

"Hullo, you chaps," said Stanning.

The members of the senior day-room made no reply, but continued, as Mr Kipling has it, to persecute their vocations. Most of them were brewing. They went on brewing with the earnest concentration of *chefs*.

"You're a cheery lot," said Stanning. "But I don't wonder you've got the hump. I should be a bit sick if we'd got a skunk like that in our house. Heard the latest?"

Some lunatic said, "No. What?" thereby delivering the day-room bound into the hands of the enemy.

"Sheen's apologised to Attell."

There was a sensation in the senior day-room, as Stanning had expected. He knew his men. He was perfectly aware that any story which centred round Sheen's cowardice would be believed by them, so he had not troubled to invent a lie which it would be difficult to disprove. He knew that in the

present state of feeling in the house Sheen would not be
given a hearing.

"No!" shouted the senior day-room.

This was the last straw. The fellow seemed to go out of
his way to lower the prestige of the house.

"Fact," said Stanning. "I thought you knew."

He continued to sit on the table, swinging his legs, while
the full horror of his story sunk into the senior day-room
mind.

"I wonder you don't do something about it. Why don't
you touch him up? He's not a prefect."

But they were not prepared to go to that length. The
senior day-room had a great respect both for Drummond's
word and his skill with his hands. He had said he would
slay any one who touched Sheen, and they were of opinion
that he would do it.

"He isn't in," said one of the brewers, looking up from his
toasting-fork. "His study door was open when I passed."

"I say, why not rag his study?" suggested another thickly,
through a mouthful of toast.

Stanning smiled.

"Good idea," he said.

It struck him that some small upheaval of Sheen's study
furniture, coupled with the burning of one or two books,
might check to some extent that student's work for the
Gotford. And if Sheen could be stopped working for the
Gotford, he, Stanning, would romp home. In the matter of
brilliance there was no comparison between them. It was
Sheen's painful habit of work which made him dangerous.

Linton had been listening to this conversation in silence.
He had come to the senior day-room to borrow a book. He
now slipped out, and made his way to Drummond's study.

Drummond was in. Linton proceeded to business.

"I say, Drummond."

"Hullo?"

"That man Stanning has come in. He's getting the senior
day-room to rag Sheen's study."

"What!"

Linton repeated his statement.

"Does the man think he owns the house?" said Drummond. "Where is he?"

"Coming up now. I hear them. What are you going to do? Stop them?"

"What do you think? Of course I am. I'm not going to have any of Appleby's crew coming into Seymour's and ragging studies."

"This ought to be worth seeing," said Linton. "Look on me as 'Charles, his friend'. I'll help if you want me, but it's your scene."

Drummond opened his door just as Stanning and his myrmidons were passing it.

"Hullo, Stanning," he said.

Stanning turned. The punitive expedition stopped.

"Do you want anything?" inquired Drummond politely.

The members of the senior day-room who were with Stanning rallied round, silent and interested. This dramatic situation appealed to them. They had a passion for rows, and this looked distinctly promising.

There was a pause. Stanning looked carefully at Drummond. Drummond looked carefully at Stanning.

"I was going to see Sheen," said Stanning at length.

"He isn't in."

"Oh!"

Another pause.

"Was it anything special?" inquired Drummond pleasantly.

The expedition edged a little forward.

"No. Oh, no. Nothing special," said Stanning.

The expedition looked disappointed.

"Any message I can give him?" asked Drummond.

"No, thanks," said Stanning.

"Sure?"

"Quite, thanks."

"I don't think it's worth while your waiting. He may not be in for some time."

"No, perhaps not. Thanks. So long."

"So long."

Stanning turned on his heel, and walked away down the

passage. Drummond went back into his study, and shut the door.

The expedition, deprived of its commander-in-chief, paused irresolutely outside. Then it followed its leader's example.

There was peace in the passage.

XV

THE ROUT AT RIPTON

On the Saturday following this episode, the first fifteen travelled to Ripton to play the return match with that school on its own ground. Of the two Ripton matches, the one played at Wrykyn was always the big event of the football year; but the other came next in importance, and the telegram which was despatched to the school shop at the close of the game was always awaited with anxiety. This year Wrykyn looked forward to the return match with a certain amount of apathy, due partly to the fact that the school was in a slack, unpatriotic state, and partly to the hammering the team had received in the previous term, when the Ripton centre three-quarters had run through and scored with monotonous regularity. "We're bound to get sat on," was the general verdict of the school.

Allardyce, while thoroughly agreeing with this opinion, did his best to conceal the fact from the rest of the team. He had certainly done his duty by them. Every day for the past fortnight the forwards and outsides had turned out to run and pass, and on the Saturdays there had been matches with Corpus, Oxford, and the Cambridge Old Wrykinians. In both games the school had been beaten. In fact, it seemed as if they could only perform really well when they had no opponents. To see the three-quarters racing down the field (at practice) and scoring innumerable (imaginary) tries, one was apt to be misled into considering them a fine quartette. But when there was a match, all the beautiful dash and precision of the passing faded away, and the last thing they did was to run straight. Barry was the only one of the four who played the game properly.

But, as regarded condition, there was nothing wrong with

the team. Even Trevor could not have made them train harder; and Allardyce in his more sanguine moments had a shadowy hope that the Ripton score might, with care, be kept in the teens.

Barry had bought a *Sportsman* at the station, and he unfolded it as the train began to move. Searching the left-hand column of the middle page, as we all do when we buy the *Sportsman* on Saturday—to see how our names look in print, and what sort of a team the enemy has got—he made a remarkable discovery. At the same moment Drummond, on the other side of the carriage, did the same.

"I say," he said, "they must have had a big clear-out at Ripton. Have you seen the team they've got out today?"

"I was just looking at it," said Barry.

"What's up with it? inquired Allardyce. "Let's have a look."

"They've only got about half their proper team. They've got a different back—Grey isn't playing."

"Both their centres are, though," said Drummond.

"More fun for us, Drum., old chap," said Attell. "I'm going home again. Stop the train."

Drummond said nothing. He hated Attell most when he tried to be facetious.

"Dunn isn't playing, nor is Waite," said Barry, "so they haven't got either of their proper halves. I say, we might have a chance of doing something today."

"Of course we shall," said Allardyce. "You've only got to buck up and we've got them on toast."

The atmosphere in the carriage became charged with optimism. It seemed a simple thing to defeat a side which was practically a Ripton "A" team. The centre three-quarters were there still, it was true, but Allardyce and Drummond ought to be able to prevent the halves ever getting the ball out to them. The team looked on those two unknown halves as timid novices, who would lose their heads at the kick-off. As a matter of fact, the system of football teaching at Ripton was so perfect, and the keenness so great, that the second fifteen was nearly as good as the first every year. But the Wrykyn team did not know this, with the exception of Allardyce, who kept his knowledge to himself; and they arrived at Ripton jaunty and confident.

Keith, the Ripton captain, who was one of the centre three-quarters who had made so many holes in the Wrykyn defence in the previous term, met the team at the station, and walked up to the school with them, carrying Allardyce's bag.

"You seem to have lost a good many men at Christmas," said Allardyce. "We were reading the *Sportsman* in the train. Apparently, you've only got ten of your last term's lot. Have they all left?"

The Ripton captain grinned ruefully.

"Not much," he replied. "They're all here. All except Dunn. You remember Dunn? Little thick-set chap who played half. He always had his hair quite tidy and parted exactly in the middle all through the game."

"Oh, yes, I remember Dunn. What's he doing now?"

"Gone to Coopers Hill. Rot, his not going to the Varsity. He'd have walked into his blue."

Allardyce agreed. He had marked Dunn in the match of the previous term, and that immaculate sportsman had made things not a little warm for him.

"Where are all the others, then?" he asked. "Where's that other half of yours? And the rest of the forwards?"

"Mumps," said Keith.

"What!"

"It's a fact. Rot, isn't it? We've had a regular bout of it. Twenty fellows got it altogether. Naturally, four of those were in the team. That's the way things happen. I only wonder the whole scrum didn't have it."

"What beastly luck," said Allardyce. "We had measles like that a couple of years ago in the summer term, and had to play the Incogs and Zingari with a sort of second eleven. We got mopped."

"That's what we shall get this afternoon, I'm afraid," said Keith.

"Oh, no," said Allardyce. "Of course you won't."

4—TWF * *

And, as events turned out, that was one of the truest
remarks he had ever made in his life.

One of the drawbacks to playing Ripton on its own
ground was the crowd. Another was the fact that one
generally got beaten. But your sportsman can put up with
defeat. What he does not like is a crowd that regards him as
a subtle blend of incompetent idiot and malicious scoundrel,
and says so very loud and clear. It was not, of course, the
school that did this. They spent their time blushing for the
shouters. It was the patriotic inhabitants of Ripton town
who made the school wish that they could be saved from
their friends. The football ground at Ripton was at the edge
of the school fields, separated from the road by narrow iron
railings; and along these railings the choicest spirits of the
town would line up, and smoke and yell, and spit and yell
again. As Wordsworth wrote, "There are two voices".
They were on something like the following lines.

Inside the railings: "Sch-oo-oo-oo-oo-l! Buck up
Sch-oo-oo-oo-oo-l!! Get it OUT, Schoo-oo-oo-oo-l!!!"

Outside the railings: "Gow it, Ripton! That's the way,
Ripton! Twist his good-old-English-adjectived neck, Rip-
ton! Sit on his forcibly described head, Ripton! Gow it,
Ripton! Haw, Haw, Haw! They ain't no use, RIPTON!
Kick 'im in the eye, RIPTON! Haw, Haw, Haw!

The bursts of merriment signalised the violent downfall
of some dangerous opponent.

The school loathed these humble supporters, and
occasionally fastidious juniors would go the length of throwing chunks of mud at them through the railings. But nothing
discouraged them or abated their fervid desire to see the
school win. Every year they seemed to increase in zeal, and
they were always in great form at the Wrykyn match.

It would be charitable to ascribe to this reason the grue-
some happenings of that afternoon. They needed some
explaining away.

Allardyce won the toss, and chose to start downhill, with
the wind in his favour. It is always best to get these advan-

tages at the beginning of the game. If one starts against the wind, it usually changes ends at half-time. Amidst a roar from both touch-lines and a volley of howls from the road, a Ripton forward kicked off. The ball flew in the direction of Stanning, on the right wing. A storm of laughter arose from the road as he dropped it. The first scrum was formed on the Wrykyn twenty-five line.

The Ripton forwards got the ball, and heeled with their usual neatness. The Ripton half who was taking the scrum gathered it cleanly, and passed to his colleague. He was a sturdy youth with a dark, rather forbidding face, in which the acute observer might have read signs of the savage. He was of the breed which is vaguely described at public schools as "nigger", a term covering every variety of shade from ebony to light lemon. As a matter of fact he was a half-caste, sent home to England to be educated. Drummond recognised him as he dived forward to tackle him. The last place where they had met had been the roped ring at Aldershot. It was his opponent in the final of the Feathers.

He reached him as he swerved, and they fell together. The ball bounded forward.

"Hullo, Peteiro," he said. "Thought you'd left."

The other grinned recognition.

"Hullo, Drummond."

"Going up to Aldershot this year?"

"Yes. Light-Weight."

"So am I."

The scrum had formed by now, and further conversation was impossible. Drummond looked a little thoughtful as he put the ball in. He had been told that Peteiro was leaving Ripton at Christmas. It was a nuisance his being still at school. Drummond was not afraid of him—he would have fought a champion of the world if the school had expected him to—but he could not help remembering that it was only by the very narrowest margin, and after a terrific three rounds, that he had beaten him in the Feathers the year before. It would be too awful for words if the decision were to be reversed in the coming competition.

But he was not allowed much leisure for pondering on

the future. The present was too full of incident and excitement. The withdrawal of the four invalids and the departure of Dunn had not reduced the Ripton team to that wreck of its former self which the Wrykyn fifteen had looked for. On the contrary, their play seemed, if anything, a shade better than it had been in the former match. There was all the old aggressiveness, and Peteiro and his partner, so far from being timid novices and losing their heads, eclipsed the exhibition given at Wrykyn by Waite and Dunn. Play had only been in progress six minutes when Keith, taking a pass on the twenty-five line, slipped past Attell, ran round the back, and scored between the posts. Three minutes later the other Ripton centre scored. At the end of twenty minutes the Wrykyn line had been crossed five times, and each of the tries had been converted.

"*Can't* you fellows get that ball in the scrum?" demanded Allardyce plaintively, as the team began for the fifth time the old familiar walk to the half-way line. "Pack tight, and get the first shove."

The result of this address was to increase the Ripton lead by four points. In his anxiety to get the ball, one of the Wrykyn forwards started heeling before it was in, and the referee promptly gave a free kick to Ripton for "foot up". As this event took place within easy reach of the Wrykyn goal, and immediately in front of the same, Keith had no difficulty in bringing off the penalty.

By half-time the crowd in the road, hoarse with laughter, had exhausted all their adjectives and were repeating themselves. The Ripton score was six goals, a penalty goal, and two tries to *nil,* and the Wrykyn team was a demoralised rabble.

The fact that the rate of scoring slackened somewhat after the interval may be attributed to the disinclination of the Riptonians to exert themselves unduly. They ceased playing in the stern and scientific spirit in which they had started; and, instead of adhering to an orthodox game, began to enjoy themselves. The forwards no longer heeled like a machine. They broke through ambitiously, and tried to score on their own account. When the outsides got as far as the back, they did not pass. They tried to drop goals. In this way only twenty-two points were scored after half-time. Allardyce and Drummond battled on nobly, but with their pack hopelessly outclassed it was impossible for them to do anything of material use. Barry, on the wing, tackled his man whenever the latter got the ball, but, as a rule, the centres did not pass, but attacked by themselves. At last, by way of a fitting conclusion to the rout, the Ripton back, catching a high punt, ran instead of kicking, and, to the huge delight of the town contingent, scored. With this incident the visiting team drained the last dregs of the bitter cup. Humiliation could go no further. Almost immediately afterwards the referee blew his whistle for "No side".

"Three cheers for Wrykyn," said Keith.

To the fifteen victims it sounded ironical.

XVI

Drummond Goes Into Retirement

The return journey of a school team after a crushing defeat
in a foreign match is never a very exhilarating business.
Those members of the side who have not yet received their
colours are wondering which of them is to be sacrificed to
popular indignation and "chucked" : the rest, who have
managed to get their caps, are feeling that even now two-
thirds of the school will be saying that they are not worth a
place in the third fifteen; while the captain, brooding apart,
is becoming soured at the thought that Posterity will forget
what little good he may have done, and remember only that
it was in his year that the school got so many points taken off
them by So-and-So. Conversation does not ripple and
sparkle during these home-comings. The Wrykyn team made
the journey in almost unbroken silence. They were all stiff
and sore, and their feelings were such as to unfit them for
talking to people.

The school took the thing very philosophically—a bad
sign. When a school is in a healthy, normal condition, it
should be stirred up by a bad defeat by another school, like
a disturbed wasps' nest. Wrykyn made one or two remarks
about people who could not play footer for toffee, and then
let the thing drop.

Sheen was too busy with his work and his boxing to have
much leisure for mourning over this latest example of the
present inefficiency of the school. The examination for the
Gotford was to come off in two days, and the inter-house
boxing was fixed for the following Wednesday. In five days,
therefore, he would get his chance of retrieving his lost place
in the school. He was certain that he could, at any rate make
a very good show against anyone in the school, even Drummond. Joe Bevan was delighted with his progress, and

quoted Shakespeare volubly in his admiration. Jack Bruce
and Francis added their tribute, and the knife and boot boy
paid him the neatest compliment of all by refusing point-
blank to have any more dealings with him whatsoever. His
professional duties, explained the knife and boot boy, did
not include being punched in the heye by blokes, and he
did not intend to be put upon.

"You'll do all right," said Jack Bruce, as they were
motoring home, "if they'll let you go in for it all. But how
do you know they will? Have they chosen the men yet?"

"Not yet. They don't do it till the day before. But there
won't be any difficulty about that. Drummond will let
me have a shot if he thinks I'm good enough."

"Oh, you're good enough," said Bruce.

And when, on Monday evening, Francis, on receipt of no
fewer than four blows in a single round—a record, shook
him by the hand and said that if ever he happened to want
a leetle darg that was a perfect bag of tricks and had got a
pedigree, mind you, he, Francis, would be proud to supply
that animal, Sheen felt that the moment had come to approach Drummond on the subject of the house boxing. It
would be a little awkward at first, and conversation would
probably run somewhat stiffly; but all would be well once he
had explained himself.

But things had been happening in his absence which
complicated the situation. Allardyce was having tea with
Drummond, who had been stopping in with a sore throat.
He had come principally to make arrangements for the
match between his house and Seymour's in the semi-final
round of the competition.

"You're looking bad," he said, taking a seat.

"I'm feeling bad," said Drummond. For the past few days
he had been very much out of sorts. He put it down to a
chill caught after the Ripton match. He had never mustered
up sufficient courage to sponge himself with cold water after
soaking in a hot bath, and he occasionally suffered for it.

"What's up?" inquired Allardyce.

"Oh, I don't know. Sort of beastly feeling. Sore throat.
Nothing much. Only it makes you feel rather rotten."

Allardyce looked interested.

"I say," he said, "it looks as if—I wonder. I hope you haven't."

"What?"

"Mumps. It sounds jolly like it."

"Mumps! Of course I've not. Why should I?"

Allardyce produced a letter from his pocket. "I got this from Keith, the Ripton captain, this morning. You know they've had a lot of the thing there. Oh, didn't you? That was why they had such a bad team out."

"Bad team!" murmured Drummond.

"Well, I mean not their best team. They had four of their men down with mumps. Here's what Keith says. Listen. Bit about hoping we got back all right, and so on, first. Then he says—here it is, 'Another of our fellows has got the mumps. One of the forwards; rather a long man who was good out of touch. He developed it a couple of days after the match. It's lucky that all our card games are over. We beat John's, Oxford, last Wednesday, and that finished the card. But it'll rather rot up the House matches. We should have walked the cup, but there's no knowing what will happen now. I hope none of your lot caught the mumps from Browning during the game. It's quite likely, of course. Browning ought not to have been playing, but I had no notion that there was anything wrong with him. He never said he felt bad.' You've got it, Drummond. That's what's the matter with you."

"Oh, rot," said Drummond. "It's only a chill."

But the school doctor, who had looked in at the house to dose a small Seymourite who had indulged too heartily in the pleasures of the table, had other views, and before lock-up Drummond was hurried off to the infirmary.

Sheen went to Drummond's study after preparation had begun, and was surprised to find him out. Not being on speaking terms with a single member of the house, he was always out-of-date as regarded items of school news. As a rule he had to wait until Jack Bruce told him before learning of any occurrence of interest. He had no notion that mumps was the cause of Drummond's absence, and he sat

and waited patiently for him in his study till the bell rang
for prayers. The only possible explanation that occurred to
him was that Drummond was in somebody else's study, and
he could not put his theory to the test by going and looking.
It was only when Drummond did not put in an appearance
at prayers that Sheen began to suspect that something might
have happened.

It was maddening not to be able to make inquiries. He
had almost decided to go and ask Linton, and risk whatever
might be the consequences of such a step, when he remembered that the matron must know. He went to her, and was
told that Drummond was in the infirmary.

He could not help seeing that this made his position a
great deal more difficult. In ten minutes he could have explained matters to Drummond if he had found him in his
study. But it would be a more difficult task to put the thing
clearly in a letter.

Meanwhile, it was bed-time, and he soon found his hands
too full with his dormitory to enable him to think out the
phrasing of that letter. The dormitory, which was recruited
entirely from the junior day-room, had heard of Drummond's departure with rejoicings. They liked Drummond,
but he was a good deal too fond of the iron hand for their
tastes. A night with Sheen in charge should prove a welcome
change.

A deafening uproar was going on when Sheen arrived,
and as he came into the room somebody turned the gas out.
He found some matches on the chest of drawers, and lit it
again just in time to see a sportive youth tearing the clothes
off his bed and piling them on the floor. A month before
he would not have known how to grapple with such a
situation, but his evenings with Joe Bevan had given him
the habit of making up his mind and acting rapidly. Drummond was wont to keep a swagger-stick by his bedside for
the better observance of law and order. Sheen possessed
himself of this swagger-stick, and reasoned with the sportive
youth. The rest of the dormitory looked on in interested
silence. It was a critical moment, and on his handling of it
depended Sheen's victory or defeat. If he did not keep his

head he was lost. A domitory is merciless to a prefect whose weakness they have discovered.

Sheen kept his head. In a quiet, pleasant voice, fingering the swagger-stick, as he spoke, in an absent manner, he requested his young friend to re-make the bed—rapidly and completely. For the space of five minutes no sound broke the silence except the rustle of sheets and blankets. At the end of that period the bed looked as good as new.

"Thanks," said Sheen gratefully. "That's very kind of you."

He turned to the rest of the dormitory.

"Don't let me detain you," he said politely. "Get into bed as soon as you like."

The dormitory got into bed sooner than they liked. For some reason the colossal rag they had planned had fizzled out. They were thoughtful as they crept between the sheets. Could these things be?

After much deliberation Sheen sent his letter to Drummond on the following day. It was not a long letter, but it was carefully worded. It explained that he had taken up boxing of late, and ended with a request that he might be allowed to act as Drummond's understudy in the House competitions.

It was late that evening when the infirmary attendant came over with the answer.

Like the original letter, the answer was brief.

"Dear Sheen," wrote Drummond, "thanks for the offer. I am afraid I can't accept it. We must have the best man. Linton is going to box for the House in the Light-Weights."

XVII

This polite epistle, it may be mentioned, was a revised version of the one which Drummond originally wrote in reply to Sheen's request. His first impulse had been to answer in the four brief words, "Don't be a fool"; for Sheen's letter had struck him as nothing more than a contemptible piece of posing, and he had all the hatred for poses which is a characteristic of the plain and straightforward type of mind. It seemed to him that Sheen, as he expressed it to himself, was trying to "do the boy hero". In the school library, which had been stocked during the dark ages, when that type of story was popular, there were numerous school stories in which the hero retrieved a rocky reputation by thrashing the bully, displaying in the encounter an intuitive but overwhelming skill with his fists. Drummond could not help feeling that Sheen must have been reading one of these stories. It was all very fine and noble of him to want to show that he was No Coward After All, like Leo Cholmondeley or whatever his beastly name was, in *The Lads of St. Ethelberta's* or some such piffling book; but, thought Drummond in his cold, practical way, what about the house? If Sheen thought that Seymour's was going to chuck away all chance of winning one of the inter-house events, simply in order to give him an opportunity of doing the Young Hero, the sooner he got rid of that sort of idea, the better. If he wanted to do the Leo Cholmondeley business, let him go and chuck a kid into the river, and jump in and save him. But he wasn't going to have the house let in for twenty Sheens.

Such were the meditations of Drummond when the infirmary attendant brought Sheen's letter to him; and he seized pencil and paper and wrote, "Don't be a fool". But pity succeeded contempt, and he tore up the writing. After all, however much he had deserved it, the man had had a bad time. It was no use jumping on him. And at one time they had been pals. Might as well do the thing politely.

All of which reflections would have been prevented had Sheen thought of mentioning the simple fact that it was Joe Bevan who had given him the lessons to which he referred in his letter. But he had decided not to do so, wishing to avoid long explanations. And there was, he felt, a chance that the letter might come into other hands than those of Drummond. So he had preserved silence on that point, thereby wrecking his entire scheme.

It struck him that he might go to Linton, explain his position, and ask him to withdraw in his favour, but there were difficulties in the way of that course. There is a great deal of red tape about the athletic arrangements of a house at a public school. When once an order has gone forth, it is difficult to get it repealed. Linton had been chosen to represent the house in the Light-Weights, and he would carry out orders. Only illness would prevent him appearing in the ring.

Sheen made up his mind not to try to take his place, and went through the days a victim to gloom, which was caused by other things besides his disappointment respecting the boxing competition. The Gotford examination was over now, and he was not satisfied with his performance. Though he did not know it, his dissatisfaction was due principally to the fact that, owing to his isolation, he had been unable to compare notes after the examinations with the others. Doing an examination without comparing notes subsequently with one's rivals, is like playing golf against a bogey. The imaginary rival against whom one pits oneself never makes a mistake. Our own "howlers" stand out in all their horrid nakedness; but we do not realise that our rivals have probably made others far worse. In this way Sheen plumbed the depths of depression. The Gotford was a purely Classical examination, with the exception of one paper, a General Knowledge paper; and it was in this that Sheen fancied he had failed so miserably. His Greek and Latin verse were always good; his prose, he felt, was not altogether beyond the pale; but in the General Knowledge paper he had come down heavily. As a matter of fact, if he had only known, the paper was an exceptionally hard one, and there was not a single candidate for the scholarship who felt satisfied with his treatment of it. It was to questions ten, eleven, and thirteen of this paper that Cardew, of the School House, who had entered for the scholarship for the sole reason that competitors got excused two clear days of ordinary school-work, wrote the following answer :

See "Encylopædia Britannica," *Times* edition.

If they really wanted to know, he said subsequently, that was the authority to go to. He himself would probably misinform them altogether.

In addition to the Gotford and the House Boxing, the House Fives now came on, and the authorities of Seymour's were in no small perplexity. They met together in Rigby's study to discuss the matter. Their difficulty was this. There was only one inmate of Seymour's who had a chance of carrying off the House Fives Cup. And that was Sheen. The house was asking itself what was to be done about it.

"You see," said Rigby, "you can look at it in two ways, whichever you like. We ought certainly to send in our best man for the pot, whatever sort of chap he is. But then, come to think of it, Sheen can't very well be said to belong to the house at all. When a man's been cut dead during the whole term, he can't be looked on as one of the house very well. See what I mean?"

"Of course he can't," said Mill, who was second in command at Seymour's. Mill's attitude towards his fellow men was one of incessant hostility. He seemed to bear a grudge against the entire race.

Rigby resumed. He was a pacific person, and hated anything resembling rows in the house. He had been sorry for Sheen, and would have been glad to give him a chance of setting himself on his legs again.

"You see." he said, "this is what I mean. We either recognise Sheen's existence or we don't. Follow? We can't get him to win this Cup for us, and then, when he has done it, go on cutting him and treating him as if he didn't belong to the house at all. I know he let the house down awfully badly in that business, but still, if he lifts the Fives Cup, that'll square the thing. If he does anything to give the house a leg-up, he must be treated as if he'd never let it down at all."

"Of course," said Barry. "I vote we send him in for the Fives."

"What rot!" said Mill. "It isn't as if none of the rest of us played fives."

"We aren't as good as Sheen," said Barry.

"I don't care. I call it rot letting a chap like him represent the house at anything. If he were the best fives-player in the world I wouldn't let him play for the house."

Rigby was impressed by his vehemence. He hesitated.

"After all, Barry," he said, "I don't know. Perhaps it might—you see, he did—well, I really think we'd better have somebody else. The house has got its knife into Sheen too much just at present to want him as a representative. There'd only be sickness, don't you think? Who else is there?"

So it came about that Menzies was chosen to uphold the house in the Fives Courts. Sheen was not surprised. But it was not pleasant. He was certainly having bad luck in his attempts to do something for the house. Perhaps if he won the Gotford they might show a little enthusiasm. The Gotford always caused a good deal of interest in the school. It was the best thing of its kind in existence at Wrykyn, and even the most abandoned loafers liked to feel that their house had won it. It was just possible, thought Sheen, that a brilliant win might change the feelings of Seymour's towards him. He did not care for the applause of the multitude more than a boy should, but he preferred it very decidedly to the cut direct.

Things went badly for Seymour's. Never in the history of the house, or, at any rate, in the comparatively recent history of the house, had there been such a slump in athletic trophies. To begin with, they were soundly beaten in the semi-

final for the House football cup by Allardyce's lot. With
Drummond away, there was none to mark the captain of the
School team at half, and Allardyce had raced through in
a manner that must have compensated him to a certain
extent for the poor time he had had in first fifteen matches.
The game had ended in a Seymourite defeat by nineteen
points to five.

Nor had the Boxing left the house in a better position.
Linton fought pluckily in the Light-Weights, but went down
before Stanning, after beating a representative of Templar's.
Mill did not show up well in the Heavy-Weights, and was
defeated in his first bout. Seymour's were reduced to telling
themselves how different it all would have been if Drummond had been there.

Sheen watched the Light-Weight contests, and nearly
danced with irritation. He felt that he could have eaten
Stanning. The man was quick with his left, but he couldn't
box. He hadn't a notion of side-stepping, and the upper-cut
appeared to be entirely outside his range. He would like to
see him tackle Francis.

Sheen thought bitterly of Drummond. Why on earth
couldn't he have given him a chance. It was maddening.

The Fives carried on the story. Menzies was swamped by
a Day's man. He might just as well have stayed away altogether. The star of Seymour's was very low on the horizon.

And then the house scored its one success. The headmaster announced it in the Hall after prayers in his dry,
unemotional way.

"I have received the list of marks," he said, "from the
examiners for the Gotford Scholarship." He paused. Sheen
felt a sudden calm triumph flood over him. Somehow,
intuitively, he knew that he had won. He waited without
excitement for the next words.

"Out of a possible thousand marks, Sheen, who wins the
scholarship, obtained seven hundred and one, Stanning six
hundred and four, Wilson . . ."

Sheen walked out of the Hall in the unique position of a
Gotford winner with only one friend to congratulate him.

Jack Bruce was the one. The other six hundred and thirty-three members of the school made no demonstration.

There was a pleasant custom at Seymour's of applauding at tea any Seymourite who had won distinction, and so shed a reflected glory on the house. The head of the house would observe, "Well played, So-and-So!" and the rest of the house would express their emotion in the way that seemed best to them, to the subsequent exultation of the local crockery merchant, who had generally to supply at least a dozen fresh cups and plates to the house after one of these occasions. When it was for getting his first eleven or first fifteen cap that the lucky man was being cheered, the total of breakages sometimes ran into the twenties.

Rigby, good, easy man, was a little doubtful as to what course to pursue in the circumstances. Should he give the signal? After all, the fellow *had* won the Gotford. It was a score for the house, and they wanted all the scores they could get in these lean years. Perhaps, then, he had better.

"Well played, Sheen," said he.

There was a dead silence. A giggle from the fags' table showed that the comedy of the situation was not lost on the young mind.

The head of the house looked troubled. This was awfully awkward.

"Well played, Sheen," he said again.

"Don't mention it, Rigby," said the winner of the Gotford politely, looking up from his plate.

XVIII

MR BEVAN MAKES A SUGGESTION

When one has been working hard with a single end in view, the arrival and departure of the supreme moment is apt to leave a feeling of emptiness, as if life had been drained of all its interest, and left nothing sufficiently exciting to make it worth doing. Horatius, as he followed his plough on a warm day over the corn land which his gratified country bestowed on him for his masterly handling of the traffic on the bridge, must sometimes have felt it was a little tame. The feeling is far more acute when one has been unexpectedly baulked in one's desire for action. Sheen, for the first few days after he received Drummond's brief note, felt that it was useless for him to try to do anything. The Fates were against him. In stories, as Mr Anstey has pointed out, the hero is never long without his chance of retrieving his reputation. A mad bull comes into the school grounds, and he alone (the hero, not the bull) is calm. Or there is a fire, and whose is that pale and gesticulating form at the upper window? The bully's, of course. And who is that climbing nimbly up the Virginia creeper? Why, the hero. Who else? Three hearty cheers for the plucky hero.

But in real life opportunities of distinguishing oneself are less frequent.

Sheen continued his visits to the "Blue Boar", but more because he shrank from telling Joe Bevan that all his trouble had been for nothing, than because he had any definite object in view. It was bitter to listen to the eulogies of the pugilist, when all the while he knew that, as far as any immediate results were concerned, it did not really matter whether he boxed well or feebly. Some day, perhaps, as Mr Bevan was fond of pointing out when he approached the subject of disadvantages of boxing, he might meet a hooligan when he was crossing a field with his sister; but he found that but small consolation. He was in the position of one who wants a small sum of ready money, and is told that, in a few years, he may come into a fortune. By the time he got a chance of proving himself a man with his hands, he would be an Old Wrykinian. He was leaving at the end of the summer term.

Jack Bruce was sympathetic, and talked more freely than was his wont.

"I can't understand it," he said. "Drummond always seemed a good sort. I should have thought he would have sent you in for the house like a shot. Are you sure you put it plainly in your letter? What did you say?"

Sheen repeated the main points of his letter.

"Did you tell him who had been teaching you?"

"No. I just said I'd been boxing lately."

"Pity," said Jack Bruce. "If you'd mentioned that it was Joe who'd been training you, he would probably have been much more for it. You see, he couldn't know whether you were any good or not from your letter. But if you'd told him that Joe Bevan and Hunt both thought you good, he'd have seen there was something in it."

"It never occurred to me. Like a fool, I was counting on the thing so much that it didn't strike me there would be any real difficulty in getting him to see my point. Especially when he got mumps and couldn't go in himself. Well, it can't be helped now."

And the conversation turned to the prospects of Jack Bruce's father in the forthcoming election, the polling for which had just begun.

"I'm busy now," said Bruce. "I'm not sure that I shall be able to do much sparring with you for a bit."

"My dear chap, don't let me—"

"Oh, it's all right, really. Taking you to the 'Blue Boar' doesn't land me out of my way at all. Most of the work lies round in this direction. I call at cottages, and lug oldest inhabitants to the poll. It's rare sport."

"Does your pater know?"

"Oh, yes. He rots me about it like anything, but, all the

same, I believe he's really rather bucked because I've roped in quite a dozen voters who wouldn't have stirred a yard if I hadn't turned up. That's where we're scoring. Pedder hasn't got a car yet, and these old rotters round here aren't going to move out of their chairs to go for a ride in an ordinary cart. But they chuck away their crutches and hop into a motor like one o'clock."

"It must be rather a rag," said Sheen.

The car drew up at the door of the "Blue Boar". Sheen got out and ran upstairs to the gymnasium. Joe Bevan was sparring a round with Francis. He watched them while he changed, but without the enthusiasm of which he had been conscious on previous occasions. The solid cleverness of Joe Bevan, and the quickness and cunning of the bantam-weight, were as much in evidence as before, but somehow the glamour and romance which had surrounded them were gone. He no longer watched eagerly to pick up the slightest hint from these experts. He felt no more interest than he would have felt in watching a game of lawn tennis. He *had* been keen. Since his disappointment with regard to the House Boxing he had become indifferent.

Joe Bevan noticed this before he had been boxing with him a minute.

"Hullo, sir," he said, "what's this? Tired today? Not feeling well? You aren't boxing like yourself, not at all you aren't. There's no weight behind 'em. You're tapping. What's the matter with your feet, too? You aren't getting about as quickly as I should like to see. What have you been doing to yourself?"

"Nothing that I know of," said Sheen. "I'm sorry I'm so rotten. Let's have another try."

The second try proved as unsatisfactory as the first. He was listless, and his leads and counters lacked conviction.

Joe Bevan, who identified himself with his pupils with that thoroughness which is the hall-mark of the first-class boxing instructor, looked so pained at his sudden loss of form, that Sheen could not resist the temptation to confide in him. After all, he must tell him some time.

"The fact is," he said, as they sat on the balcony

overlooking the river, waiting for Jack Bruce to return with his car, "I've had a bit of a sickener."

"I thought you'd got sick of it," said Mr Bevan. "Well, have a bit of a rest."

"I don't mean that I'm tired of boxing," Sheen hastened to explain. "After all the trouble you've taken with me, it would be a bit thick if I chucked it just as I was beginning to get on. It isn't that. But you know how keen I was on boxing for the house?"

Joe Bevan nodded.

"Did you get beat?"

"They wouldn't let me go in," said Sheen.

"But, bless me! you'd have made babies of them. What was the instructor doing? Couldn't he see that you were good?"

"I didn't get a chance of showing what I could do." He explained the difficulties of the situation.

Mr Bevan nodded his head thoughtfully.

"So naturally," concluded Sheen, "the thing has put me out a bit. It's beastly having nothing to work for. I'm at a loose end. Up till now, I've always had the thought of the House Competition to keep me going. But now—well, you see how it is. It's like running to catch a train, and then finding suddenly that you've got plenty of time. There doesn't seem any point in going on running."

"Why not Aldershot, sir? said Mr Bevan.

"What!" cried Sheen.

The absolute novelty of the idea, and the gorgeous possibilities of it, made him tingle from head to foot. Aldershot! Why hadn't he thought of it before! The House Competition suddenly lost its importance in his eyes. It was a trivial affair, after all, compared with Aldershot, that Mecca of the public-school boxer.

Then the glow began to fade. Doubts crept in. He might have learned a good deal from Joe Bevan, but had he learned enough to be able to hold his own with the best boxers of all the public schools in the country? And if he had the skill to win, had he the heart? Joe Bevan had said that he would not disgrace himself again, and he felt that the chances were against his doing so, but there was the terrible possibility. He had stood up to Francis and the others, and he had taken their blows without flinching; but in these encounters there was always at the back of his mind the comforting feeling that there was a limit to the amount of punishment he would receive. If Francis happened to drive him into a corner where he could neither attack, nor defend himself against attack, he did not use his advantage to the full. He indicated rather than used it. A couple of blows, and he moved out into the open again. But in the Public Schools Competition at Aldershot there would be no quarter. There would be nothing but deadly earnest. If he allowed himself to be manoeuvred into an awkward position, only his own skill, or the call of time, could extricate him from it.

In a word, at the "Blue Boar" he sparred. At Aldershot he would have to fight. Was he capable of fighting?

Then there was another difficulty. How was he to get himself appointed as the Wrykyn light-weight representative? Now that Drummond was unable to box, Stanning would go down, as the winner of the School Competition. These things were worked by an automatic process. Sheen felt that he could beat Stanning, but he had no means of publishing this fact to the school. He could not challenge him to a trial of skill. That sort of thing was not done.

He explained this to Joe Bevan.

"Well, it's a pity," said Joe regretfully. "It's a pity."

At this moment Jack Bruce appeared.

"What's a pity, Joe?" he asked.

"Jo wants me to go to Aldershot as a light-weight," explained Sheen, "and I was just saying that I couldn't, because of Stanning."

"What about Stanning?"

"He won the School Competition, you see, so they're bound to send him down."

"Half a minute," said Jack Bruce. "I never thought of Aldershot for you before. It's a jolly good idea. I believe you'd have a chance. And it's all right about Stanning. He's not going down. Haven't you heard?"

"I don't hear anything. Why isn't he going down?"

"He's knocked up one of his wrists. So he says."

"How do you mean—so he says?" asked Sheen.

"I believe he funks it."

"Why? What makes you think that?"

"Oh, I don't know. It's only my opinion. Still, it's a little queer. Stanning says he crocked his left wrist in the final of the House Competition."

"Well, what's wrong with that? Why shouldn't he have done so?"

Sheen objected strongly to Stanning, but he had the elements of justice in him, and he was not going to condemn him on insufficient evidence, particularly of a crime of which he himself had been guilty.

"Of course he may have done," said Bruce. "But it's a bit fishy that he should have been playing fives all right two days running just after the competition."

"He might have crocked himself then."

"Then why didn't he say so?"

A question which Sheen found himself unable to answer.

"Then there's nothing to prevent you fighting, sir," said Joe Bevan, who had been listening attentively to the conversation.

"Do you really think I've got a chance?"

"I do, sir."

"Of course you have," said Jack Bruce. "You're quite as good as Drummond was, last time I saw him box."

"Then I'll have a shot at it," said Sheen.

"Good for you, sir," cried Joe Bevan.

"Though it'll be a bit of a job getting leave," said Sheen. "How would you start about it, Bruce?"

"You'd better ask Spence. He's the man to go to."

"That's all right. I'm rather a pal of Spence's."

"Ask him tonight after prep.," suggested Bruce.

"And then you can come here regular," said Joe Bevan, "and we'll train you till you're that fit you could eat bricks, and you'll make babies of them up at Aldershot."

XIX

Paving the Way

Bruce had been perfectly correct in his suspicions. Stanning's wrist was no more sprained than his ankle. The advisability of manufacturing an injury had come home to him very vividly on the Saturday morning following the Ripton match, when he had read the brief report of that painful episode in that week's number of the *Field* in the school library. In the list of the Ripton team appeared the name R. Peteiro. He had heard a great deal about the dusky Riptonian when Drummond had beaten him in the Feather-Weights the year before. Drummond had returned from Aldershot on that occasion cheerful, but in an extremely battered condition. His appearance as he limped about the field on Sports Day had been heroic, and, in addition, a fine advertisment for the punishing powers of the Ripton champion. It is true that at least one of his injuries had been the work of a Pauline whom he had met in the opening bout; but the great majority were presents from Ripton, and Drummond had described the dusky one, in no uncertain terms, as a holy terror.

These things had sunk into Stanning's mind. It had been generally understood at Wrykyn that Peteiro had left school at Christmas. When Stanning, through his study of the *Field*, discovered that the redoubtable boxer had been one of the team against which he had played at Ripton, and realised that, owing to Drummond's illness, it would fall to him, if he won the House Competition, to meet this man of wrath at Aldershot, he resolved on the instant that the most persuasive of wild horses should not draw him to that military centre on the day of the Public Schools Competition. The difficulty was that he particularly wished to win the House Cup. Then it occurred to him that he could combine the two things—win the competition and get injured while doing so.

Accordingly, two days after the House Boxing he was observed to issue from Appleby's with his left arm slung in a first fifteen scarf. He was too astute to injure his right wrist. What happens to one's left wrist at school is one's own private business. When one injures one's right arm, and so incapacitates oneself for form work, the authorities begin to make awkward investigations.

Mr Spence, who looked after the school's efforts to win medals at Aldershot, was the most disappointed person in the place. He was an enthusiastic boxer—he had represented Cambridge in the Middle-Weights in his day—and with no small trouble had succeeded in making boxing a going concern at Wrykyn. Years of failure had ended, the Easter before, in a huge triumph, when O'Hara, of Dexter's and Drummond had won silver medals, and Moriarty, of Dexter's, a bronze. If only somebody could win a medal this year, the tradition would be established, and would not soon die out. Unfortunately, there was not a great deal of boxing talent in the school just now. The rule that the winner at his weight in the House Competitions should represent the school at Aldershot only applied if the winner were fairly proficient. Mr Spence exercised his discretion. It was no use sending down novices to be massacred. This year Drummond and Stanning were the only Wrykinians up to Aldershot form. Drummond would have been almost a certainty for a silver medal, and Stanning would probably have been a runner-up. And here they were, both injured; Wrykyn would not have a single representative at the Queen's Avenue Gymnasium. It would be a set-back to the cult of boxing at the school.

Mr Spence was pondering over this unfortunate state of things when Sheen was shown in.

"Can I speak to you for a minute, sir?" said Sheen.

"Certainly, Sheen. Take one of those cig—I mean, sit down. What is it?"

Sheen had decided how to open the interview before knocking at the door. He came to the point at once.

"Do you think I could go down to Aldershot, sir?" he asked.

Mr Spence looked surprised.

"Go down? You mean—? Do you want to watch the competition? Really, I don't know if the headmaster—"

"I mean, can I box?"

Mr Spence's look of surprise became more marked.

"Box?" he said. "But surely—I didn't know you were a boxer, Sheen."

"I've only taken it up lately."

"But you didn't enter for the House Competitions, did you? What weight are you?"

"Just under ten stone."

"A light-weight. Why, Linton boxed for your house in the Light-Weights surely?"

"Yes sir. They wouldn't let me go in."

"You hurt yourself?"

"No, sir."

"Then why wouldn't they let you go in?"

"Drummond thought Linton was better. He didn't know I boxed."

"But—this is very curious. I don't understand it at all. You see, if you were not up to House form, you would hardly— At Aldershot, you see, you would meet the best boxers of all the public schools."

"Yes, sir."

There was a pause.

"It was like this, sir," said Sheen nervously. "At the beginning of the term there was a bit of a row down in the town, and I got mixed up in it. And I didn't—I was afraid to join in. I funked it."

Mr Spence nodded. He was deeply interested now. The office of confessor is always interesting.

"Go on, Sheen. What happened then?"

"I was cut by everybody. The fellows thought I had let the house down, and it got about, and the other houses scored off them, so I had rather a rotten time."

Here it occurred to him that he was telling his story

without that attention to polite phraseology which a master expects from a boy, so he amended the last sentence.

"I didn't have a very pleasant time, sir," was his correction.

"Well?" said Mr Spence.

"So I was a bit sick," continued Sheen, relapsing once more into the vernacular, "and I wanted to do something to put things right again, and I met—anyhow, I took up boxing. I wanted to box for the house, if I was good enough. I practised every day, and stuck to it, and after a bit I did become pretty good."

"Well?"

"Then Drummond got mumps, and I wrote to him asking if I might represent the house instead of him, and I suppose he didn't believe I was any good. At any rate, he wouldn't let me go in. Then Joe—a man who knows something about boxing—suggested I should go down to Aldershot."

"Joe?" said Mr Spence inquiringly.

Sheen had let the name slip out unintentionally, but it was too late now to recall it.

"Joe Bevan, sir," he said. "He used to be champion of England, light-weight."

"Joe Bevan!" cried Mr Spence. "Really? Why, he trained me when I boxed for Cambridge. He's one of the best of fellows. I've never seen any one who took such trouble with his man. I wish we could get him here. So it was Joe who suggested that you should go down to Aldershot? Well, he ought to know. Did he say you would have a good chance?"

"Yes, sir."

"My position is this, you see, Sheen. There is nothing I should like more than to see the school represented at Aldershot. But I cannot let anyone go down, irrespective of his abilities. Aldershot is not child's play. And in the Light-Weights you get the hardest fighting of all. It wouldn't do for me to let you go down if you are not up to the proper form. You would be half killed."

"I should like to have a shot, sir," said Sheen.

"Then this year, as you probably know, Ripton are

sending down Peteiro for the Light-Weights. He was the fellow whom Drummond only just beat last year. And you saw the state in which Drummond came back. If Drummond could hardly hold him, what would you do?"

"I believe I could beat Drummond, sir," said Sheen.

Mr Spence's eyes opened wider. Here were brave words. This youth evidently meant business. The thing puzzled him. On the one hand, Sheen had been cut by his house for cowardice. On the other, Joe Bevan, who of all men was best able to judge, had told him that he was good enough to box at Aldershot.

"Let me think it over, Sheen," he said. "This is a matter which I cannot decide in a moment. I will tell you tomorrow what I think about it."

"I hope you will let me go down, sir," said Sheen. "It's my one chance."

"Yes, yes, I see that, I see that," said Mr Spence, "but all the same—well, I will think it over."

All the rest of that evening he pondered over the matter, deeply perplexed. It would be nothing less than cruel to let Sheen enter the ring at Aldershot if he were incompetent. Boxing in the Public Schools Boxing Competition is not a pastime for the incompetent. But he wished very much that Wrykyn should be represented, and also he sympathised with Sheen's eagerness to wipe out the stain on his honour, and the honour of the house. But, like Drummond, he could not help harbouring a suspicion that this was a pose. He felt that Sheen was intoxicated by his imagination. Every one likes to picture himself doing dashing things in the limelight, with an appreciative multitude to applaud. Would this mood stand the test of action?

Against this there was the evidence of Joe Bevan. Joe had said that Sheen was worthy to fight for his school, and Joe knew.

Mr Spence went to bed still in a state of doubt.

Next morning he hit upon a solution of the difficulty. Wandering in the grounds before school, he came upon O'Hara, who, as has been stated before, had won the Light-Weights at Aldershot in the previous year. He had come to

Wrykyn for the Sports. Here was the man to help him.
O'Hara should put on the gloves with Sheen and report.

"I'm in rather a difficulty, O'Hara," he said, "and you
can help me."

"What's that?" inquired O'Hara.

"You know both our light-weights are on the sick list?
I had just resigned myself to going down to Aldershot without any one to box, when a boy in Seymour's volunteered
for the vacant place. I don't know if you knew him at
school? Sheen. Do you remember him?"

"Sheen?" cried O'Hara in amazement. "Not *Sheen!*"...

His recollections of Sheen were not conducive to a picture
of him as a public-school boxer.

"Yes. I had never heard of him as a boxer. Still, he
seems very anxious to go down, and he certainly has one
remarkable testimonial, and as there's no one else—"

"And what shall I do?" asked O'Hara.

"I want you, if you will, to give him a trial in the dinner-
hour. Just see if he's any good at all. If he isn't, of course,
don't hit him about a great deal. But if he shows signs of
being a useful man, extend him. See what he can do."

"Very well, sir," said O'Hara.

"And you might look in at my house at tea-time, if you
have nothing better to do, and tell me what you think of
him."

At five o'clock, when he entered Mr Spence's study,
O'Hara's face wore the awe-struck look of one who had
seen visions.

"Well?" said Mr Spence. "Did you find him any good?"

"Good?" said O'Hara. "He'll beat them all. He's a
a champion. There's no stopping him."

"What an extraordinary thing! said Mr Spence.

XX

Sheen Goes to Aldershot

At Sheen's request Mr Spence made no announcement of the fact that Wrykyn would be represented in the Light-Weights. It would be time enough, Sheen felt, for the School to know that he was a boxer when he had been down and shown what he could do. His appearance in his new role would be the most surprising thing that had happened in the place for years, and it would be a painful anti-climax if, after all the excitement which would be caused by the discovery that he could use his hands, he were to be defeated in his first bout. Whereas, if he happened to win, the announcement of his victory would be all the more impressive, coming unexpectedly. To himself he did not admit the possibility of defeat. He had braced himself up for the ordeal, and he refused to acknowledge to himself that he might not come out of it well. Besides, Joe Bevan continued to express hopeful opinions.

"Just you keep your head, sir." he said, "and you'll win. Lots of these gentlemen, they're champions when they're practising, and you'd think nothing wouldn't stop them when they get into the ring. But they get wild directly they begin, and forget everything they've been taught, and where are they then? Why, on the floor, waiting for the referee to count them out."

This picture might have encouraged Sheen more if he had not reflected that he was just as likely to fall into this error as were his opponents.

"What you want to remember is to keep that guard up. Nothing can beat that. And push out your left straight. The straight left rules the boxing world. And be earnest about it. Be as friendly as you like afterwards, but while you're in the ring say to yourself, 'Well, it's you or me', and don't be too kind."

"I wish you could come down to second me, Joe," said Sheen.

"I'll have a jolly good try, sir," said Joe Bevan. "Let me see. You'll be going down the night before—I can't come down then, but I'll try and manage it by an early train on the day."

"How about Francis?"

"Oh, Francis can look after himself for one day. He's not the sort of boy to run wild if he's left alone for a few hours."

"Then you think you can manage it?"

"Yes, sir. If I'm not there for your first fight, I shall come in time to second you in the final."

"If I get there," said Sheen.

"Good seconding's half the battle. These soldiers they give you at Aldershot—well, they don't know the business, as the saying is. They don't look after their man, not like I could. I saw young what's-his-name, of Rugby—Stevens: he was beaten in the final by a gentleman from Harrow— I saw him fight there a couple of years ago. After the first round he was leading—not by much, but still, he was a point or two ahead. Well! He went to his corner and his seconds sent him up for the next round in the same state he'd got there in. They hadn't done a thing to him. Why, if I'd been in his corner I'd have taken him and sponged him and sent him up again as fresh as he could be. You must have a good second if you're to win. When you're all on top of your man, I don't say. But you get a young gentleman of your own class, just about as quick and strong as you are, and then you'll know where the seconding comes in."

"Then, for goodness' sake, don't make any mistake about coming down," said Sheen.

"I'll be there, sir," said Joe Bevan.

The Queen's Avenue Gymnasium at Aldershot is a roomy place, but it is always crowded on the Public Schools' Day. Sisters and cousins and aunts of competitors flock there to see Tommy or Bobby perform, under the impression, it is to be supposed, that he is about to take part in a pleasant frolic, a sort of merry parlour game. What their opinion is after he emerges from a warm three rounds is not known. Then there are soldiers in scores. Their views on boxing as a sport are crisp and easily defined. What they want is Gore. Others of the spectators are Old Boys, come to see how the school can behave in an emergency, and to find out whether there are still experts like Jones, who won the Middles in '96 or Robinson, who was runner-up in the Feathers in the same year; or whether, as they have darkly suspected for some time, the school has Gone To The Dogs Since They Left.

The usual crowd was gathered in the seats round the ring when Sheen came out of the dressing-room and sat down in an obscure corner at the end of the barrier which divides the gymnasium into two parts on these occasions. He felt very lonely. Mr Spence and the school instructor were watching the gymnastics, which had just started upon their lengthy course. The Wrykyn pair were not expected to figure high on the list this year. He could have joined Mr Spence, but, at the moment, he felt disinclined for conversation. If he had been a more enthusiastic cricketer, he would have recognised the feeling as that which attacks a batsman before he goes to the wicket. It is not precisely funk. It is rather a desire to accelerate the flight of Time, and get to business quickly. All things come to him who waits, and among them is that unpleasant sensation of a cold hand upon the portion of the body which lies behind the third waistcoat button.

The boxing had begun with a bout between two feather-weights, both obviously suffering from stage-fright. They were fighting in a scrambling and unscientific manner, which bore out Mr Bevan's statements on the subject of losing one's head. Sheen felt that both were capable of better things. In the second and third rounds this proved to be the case and the contest came to an end amidst applause.

The next pair were light-weights, and Sheen settled himself to watch more attentively. From these he would gather some indication of what he might expect to find when he entered the ring. He would not have to fight for some time yet. In the drawing for numbers, which had taken place in the dressing-room, he had picked a three. There would be another light-weight battle before he was called upon. His opponent was a Tonbridgian, who, from the glimpse Sheen caught of him, seemed muscular. But he (Sheen) had the advantage in reach, and built on that.

After opening tamely, the light-weight bout had become vigorous in the second round, and both men had apparently forgotten that their right arms had been given them by Nature for the purpose of guarding. They were going at it in hurricane fashion all over the ring. Sheen was horrified to feel symptoms of a return of that old sensation of panic which had caused him, on that dark day early in the term, to flee Albert and his wicked works. He set his teeth, and fought it down. And after a bad minute he was able to argue himself into a proper frame of mind again. After all, that sort of thing looked much worse than it really was. Half those blows, which seemed as if they must do tremendous damage, were probably hardly felt by their recipient. He told himself that Francis, and even the knife-and-boot boy, hit fully as hard, or harder, and he had never minded them. At the end of the contest he was once more looking forward to his entrance to the ring with proper fortitude.

The fighting was going briskly forward now, sometimes good, sometimes moderate, but always earnest, and he found himself contemplating, without undue excitement, the fact that at the end of the bout which had just begun, between middle-weights from St Paul's and Wellington, it would be his turn to perform. As luck would have it, he had not so long to wait as he had expected, for the Pauline, taking the lead after the first few exchanges, out-fought his man so completely that the referee stopped the contest in the second round. Sheen got up from his corner and went to the dressing-room. The Tonbridgian was already there. He took off his coat. Somebody crammed his hands into the gloves and from that moment the last trace of nervousness left him. He trembled with the excitement of the thing, and hoped sincerely that no one would notice it, and think that he was afraid.

Then, amidst a clapping of hands which sounded faint

and far-off, he followed his opponent to the ring, and ducked under the ropes.

The referee consulted a paper which he held, and announced the names.

"R. D. Sheen, Wrykyn College."

Sheen wriggled his fingers right into the gloves, and thought of Joe Bevan. What had Joe said? Keep that guard up. The straight left. Keep that guard—the straight left. Keep that—

"A. W. Bird, Tonbridge School."

There was a fresh outburst of applause. The Tonbridgian had shown up well in the competition of the previous year, and the crowd welcomed him as an old friend.

Keep that guard up—straight left. Straight left—guard up.

"Seconds out of the ring."

Guard up. Not too high. Straight left. It beats the world. What an age that man was calling Time. Guard up. Straight—

"Time," said the referee.

Sheen, filled with a great calm, walked out of his corner and shook hands with his opponent.

XXI

A Good Start

It was all over in half a minute.

The Tonbridgian was a two-handed fighter of the rushing type almost immediately after he had shaken hands. Sheen found himself against the ropes, blinking from a heavy hit between the eyes. Through the mist he saw his opponent sparring up to him, and as he hit he side-stepped. The next moment he was out in the middle again, with his man pressing him hard. There was a quick rally, and then Sheen swung his right at a venture. The blow had no conscious aim. It was purely speculative. But it succeeded. The Tonbridgian fell with a thud.

Sheen drew back. The thing seemed pathetic. He had braced himself up for a long fight, and it had ended in half a minute. His sensations were mixed. The fighting half of him was praying that his man would get up and start again. The prudent half realised that it was best that he should stay down. He had other fights before him before he could call that silver medal his own, and this would give him an invaluable start in the race. His rivals had all had to battle hard in their opening bouts.

The Tonbridgian's rigidity had given place to spasmodic efforts to rise. He got on one knee, and his gloved hand roamed feebly about in search of a hold. It was plain that he had shot his bolt. The referee signed to his seconds, who ducked into the ring and carried him to his corner. Sheen walked back to his own corner, and sat down. Presently the referee called out his name as the winner, and he went across the ring and shook hands with his opponent, who was now himself again.

He overheard snatches of conversation as he made his way through the crowd to the dressing-room.

"Useful boxer, that Wrykyn boy."

"Shortest fight I've seen here since Hopley won the Heavy-Weights."

"Fluke, do you think?"

"Don't know. Came to the same thing in the end, anyhow. Caught him fair."

"Hard luck on that Tonbridge man. He's a good boxer, really. Did well here last year."

Then an outburst of hand-claps drowned the speakers' voices. A swarthy youth with the Ripton pink and green on his vest had pushed past him and was entering the ring. As he entered the dressing-room he heard the referee announcing the names. So that was the famous Peteiro! Sheen admitted to himself that he looked tough, and hurried into his coat and out of the dressing-room again so as to be in time to see how the Ripton terror shaped.

It was plainly not a one-sided encounter. Peteiro's opponent hailed from St Paul's, a school that has a habit of turning out boxers. At the end of the first round it seemed that honours were even. The great Peteiro had taken as much as he had given, and once had been uncompromisingly floored by the Pauline's left. But in the second round he began to gain points. For a boy of his weight he had a terrific hit with the right, and three applications of this to the ribs early in the round took much of the sting out of the Pauline's blows. He fought on with undiminished pluck, but the Riptonian was too strong for him, and the third round was a rout. To quote the *Sportsman* of the following day, "Peteiro crowded in a lot of work with both hands, and scored a popular victory".

Sheen looked thoughtful at the conclusion of the fight. There was no doubt that Drummond's antagonist of the previous year was formidable. Yet Sheen believed himself to be the cleverer of the two. At any rate, Peteiro had given no signs of possessing much cunning. To all appearances he was a tough, go-ahead fighter, with a right which would drill a hole in a steel plate. Had he sufficient skill to baffle his (Sheen's) strong tactics? If only Joe Bevan would come! With Joe in his corner to direct him, he would feel safe.

But of Joe up to the present there were no signs.

Mr Spence came and sat down beside him.

"Well, Sheen," he said, "so you won your first fight. Keep it up."

"I'll try, sir," said Sheen.

"What do you think of Peteiro?"

"I was just wondering, sir. He hits very hard."

"Very hard indeed."

"But he doesn't look as if he was very clever."

"Not a bit. Just a plain slogger. That's all. That's why Drummond beat him last year in the Feather-Weights. In strength there was no comparison, but Drummond was just too clever for him. You will be the same, Sheen."

"I hope so, sir," said Sheen.

After lunch the second act of the performance began. Sheen had to meet a boxer from Harrow who had drawn a bye in the first round of the competition. This proved a harder fight than his first encounter, but by virtue of a stout heart and a straight left he came through it successfully, and there was no doubt as to what the decision would be. Both judges voted for him.

Peteiro demolished a Radleian in his next fight.

By the middle of the afternoon there were three light-weights in the running— Sheen, Peteiro, and a boy from Clifton. Sheen drew the bye, and sparred in an outer room with a soldier, who was inclined to take the thing easily. Sheen, with the thought of the final in his mind, was only too ready to oblige him. They sparred an innocuous three rounds, and the man of war was kind enough to whisper in his ear as they left the room that he hoped he would win the final, and that he himself had a matter of one-and-sixpence with Old Spud Smith on his success.

"For I'm a man," said the amiable warrior confidentially,

"as knows Class when he sees it. You're Class, sir, that's what you are."

This, taken in conjunction with the fact that if the worst came to the worst he had, at any rate, won a medal by having got into the final, cheered Sheen. If only Joe Bevan had appeared he would have been perfectly contented.

But there were no signs of Joe.

XXII

A Good Finish

Final, Light-Weights," shouted the referee.

A murmur of interest from the ring-side chairs.

"R. D. Sheen, Wrykyn College."

Sheen got his full measure of applause this time. His victories in the preliminary bouts had won him favour with the spectators.

"J. Peteiro, Ripton School."

"Go it, Ripton!" cried a voice from near the door. The referee frowned in the direction of this audacious partisan, and expressed a hope that the audience would kindly refrain from comment during the rounds.

Then he turned to the ring again, and announced the names a second time.

"Sheen—Peteiro."

The Ripton man was sitting with a hand on each knee, listening to the advice of his school instructor, who had thrust head and shoulders through the ropes, and was busy impressing some point upon him. Sheen found himself noticing the most trivial things with extraordinary clearness. In the front row of the spectators sat a man with a parti-coloured tie. He wondered idly what tie it was. It was rather like one worn by members of Templar's house at Wrykyn. Why were the ropes of the ring red? He rather liked the colour. There was a man lighting a pipe. Would he blow out the match or extinguish it with a wave of the hand? What a beast Peteiro looked. He really was a nigger. He must look out for that right of his. The straight left. Push it out. Straight left ruled the boxing world. Where was Joe? He must have missed the train. Or perhaps he hadn't been able to get away. Why did he want to yawn, he wondered.

"Time!"

The Ripton man became suddenly active. He almost ran across the ring. A brief handshake, and he had penned Sheen up in his corner before he had time to leave it. It was evident what advice his instructor had been giving him. He meant to force the pace from the start.

The suddenness of it threw Sheen momentarily off his balance. He seemed to be in a whirl of blows. A sharp shock from behind. He had run up against the post. Despite everything, he remembered to keep his guard up, and stopped a lashing hit from his antagonist's left. But he was too late to keep out his right. In it came, full on the weakest spot on his left side. The pain of it caused him to double up for an instant, and as he did so his opponent upper-cut him. There was no rest for him. Nothing that he had ever experienced with the gloves on approached this. If only he could get out of this corner.

Then, almost unconsciously, he recalled Joe Bevan's advice.

"If a man's got you in a corner," Joe had said, "fall on him."

Peteiro made another savage swing. Sheen dodged it and hurled himself forward.

"Break away," said a dispassionate official voice.

Sheen broke away, but now he was out of the corner with the whole good, open ring to manoeuvre in.

He could just see the Ripton instructor signalling violently to his opponent, and, in reply to the signals, Peteiro came on again with another fierce rush.

But Sheen in the open was a different person from Sheen cooped up in a corner. Francis Hunt had taught him to use his feet. He side-stepped, and, turning quickly, found his man staggering past him, over-balanced by the force of his wasted blow. And now it was Sheen who attacked, and Peteiro who tried to escape. Two swift hits he got in before his opponent could face round, and another as he turned and rushed. Then for a while the battle raged without science all over the ring. Gradually, with a cold feeling of dismay, Sheen realised that his strength was going. The pace was too hot. He could not keep it up. His left counters were losing their force. Now he was merely pushing his glove into the Ripton man's face. It was not enough. The other was getting to close quarters, and that right of his seemed stronger than ever.

He was against the ropes now, gasping for breath, and Peteiro's right was thudding against his ribs. It could not last. He gathered all his strength and put it into a straight left. It took the Ripton man in the throat, and drove him back a step. He came on again. Again Sheen stopped him.

It was his last effort. He could do no more. Everything seemed black to him. He leaned against the ropes and drank in the air in great gulps.

"Time!" said the referee.

The word was lost in the shouts that rose from the packed seats.

Sheen tottered to his corner and sat down.

"Keep it up, sir, keep it up," said a voice. "Bear't that the opposèd may beware of thee. Don't forget the guard. And the straight left beats the world."

It was Joe—at the eleventh hour.

With a delicious feeling of content Sheen leaned back in his chair. It would be all right now. He felt that the matter had been taken out of his hands. A more experienced brain than his would look after the generalship of the fight.

As the moments of the half-minute's rest slid away he discovered the truth of Joe's remarks on the value of a good second. In his other fights the flapping of the towel had hardly stirred the hair on his forehead. Joe's energetic arms set a perfect gale blowing. The cool air revived him. He opened his mouth and drank it in. A spongeful of cold water completed the cure. Long before the call of Time he was ready for the next round.

"Keep away from him, sir," said Joe, "and score with that left of yours. Don't try the right yet. Keep it for guarding. Box clever. Don't let him corner you. Slip him when he rushes. Cool and steady does it. Don't aim at his face too much. Go down below. That's the *de*-partment. And use your feet. Get about quick, and you'll find he don't like that.

Hullo, says he, I can't touch him. Then, when he's tired, go in."

The pupil nodded with closed eyes.

While these words of wisdom were proceeding from the mouth of Mr Bevan, another conversation was taking place which would have interested Sheen if he could have heard it. Mr Spence and the school instructor were watching the final from the seats under the side windows.

"It's extraordinary," said Mr Spence. "The boy's wonderfully good for the short time he has been learning. You ought to be proud of your pupil."

"Sir?"

"I was saying that Sheen does you credit."

"Not me, sir."

"What! He told me he had been taking lessons. Didn't you teach him?"

"Never set eyes on him, till this moment. Wish I had, sir. He's the sort of pupil I could wish for."

Mr Spence bent forward and scanned the features of the man who was attending the Wrykinian.

"Why," he said, "surely that's Bevan—Joe Bevan! I knew him at Cambridge."

"Yes, sir, that's Bevan," replied the instructor. "He teaches boxing at Wrykyn now, sir."

"At Wrykyn—where?"

"Up the river—at the 'Blue Boar', sir," said the instructor, quite innocently—for it did not occur to him that this simple little bit of information was just so much incriminating evidence against Sheen.

Mr Spence said nothing, but he opened his eyes very wide. Recalling his recent conversation with Sheen, he remembered that the boy had told him he had been taking lessons, and also that Joe Bevan, the ex-pugilist, had expressed a high opinion of his work. Mr Spence had imagined that Bevan had been a chance spectator of the boy's skill; but it would now seem that Bevan himself had taught Sheen. This matter, decided Mr Spence, must be looked into, for it was palpable that Sheen had broken bounds in order to attend Bevan's boxing-saloon up the river.

For the present, however, Mr Spence was content to say nothing.

Sheen came up for the second round fresh and confident. His head was clear, and his breath no longer came in gasps. There was to be no rallying this time. He had had the worst of the first round, and meant to make up his lost points.

Peteiro, losing no time, dashed in. Sheen met him with a left in the face, and gave way a foot. Again Peteiro rushed, and again he was stopped. As he bored in for the third time Sheen slipped him. The Ripton man paused, and dropped his guard for a moment.

Sheen's left shot out once more, and found its mark. Peteiro swung his right viciously, but without effect. Another swift counter added one more point to Sheen's score.

Sheen nearly chuckled. It was all so beautifully simple. What a fool he had been to mix it up in the first round. If he only kept his head and stuck to out-fighting he could win with ease. The man couldn't box. He was nothing more than a slogger. Here he came, as usual, with the old familiar rush. Out went his left. But it missed its billet. Peteiro had checked his rush after the first movement, and now he came in with both hands. It was the first time during the round that he had got to close quarters, and he made the most of it. Sheen's blows were as frequent, but his were harder. He drove at the body, right and left; and once again the call of Time extricated Sheen from an awkward position. As far as points were concerned he had had the best of the round, but he was very sore and bruised. His left side was one dull ache.

"Keep away from him, sir," said Joe Bevan. "You were ahead on that round. Keep away all the time unless he gets tired. But if you see me signalling, then go in all you can and have a fight."

There was a suspicion of weariness about the look of the Ripton champion as he shook hands for the last round. He was beginning to feel the effects of his hurricane fighting in the opening rounds. He began quietly, sparring for an opening. Sheen led with his left. Peteiro was too late with his

guard. Sheen tried again—a double lead. His opponent
guarded the first blow, but the second went home heavily
on the body, and he gave way a step.

Then from the corner of his eye Sheen saw Bevan gesticulating wildly, so, taking his life in his hands, he abandoned
his waiting game, dropped his guard, and dashed in to fight.
Peteiro met him doggedly. For a few moments the exchanges
were even. Then suddenly the Riptonian's blows began to
weaken. He got home his right on the head, and Sheen
hardly felt it. And in a flash there came to him the glorious
certainty that the game was his.

He was winning—winning—winning.

"That's enough," said the referee.

The Ripton man was leaning against the ropes, utterly
spent, at almost the same spot where Sheen had leaned at
the end of the first round. The last attack had finished him.
His seconds helped him to his corner.

The referee waved his hand.

"Sheen wins," he said.

And that was the greatest moment of his life.

XXIII

A Surprise for Seymour's

Seymour's house took in one copy of the *Sportsman* daily.
On the morning after the Aldershot competition Linton met
the paper-boy at the door on his return from the fives
courts, where he had been playing a couple of before-
breakfast games with Dunstable. He relieved him of the
house copy, and opened it to see how the Wrykyn pair had
performed in the gymnastics. He did not expect anything
great, having a rooted contempt for both experts, who were
small and, except in the gymnasium, obscure. Indeed, he
had gone so far on the previous day as to express a hope
that Biddle, the more despicable of the two, would fall off
the horizontal bar and break his neck. Still he might as well
see where they had come out. After all, with all their faults,
they were human beings like himself, and Wrykinians.

The competition was reported in the Boxing column. The
first thing that caught his eye was the name of the school
among the headlines. "Honours", said the headline, "for
St Paul's, Harrow, and Wrykyn".

"Hullo," said Linton, "what's all this?"

Then the thing came on him with nothing to soften the
shock. He had folded the paper, and the last words on the
half uppermost were, *"Final. Sheen beat Peteiro"*.

Linton had often read novels in which some important
document "swam before the eyes" of the hero or the
heroine; but he had never understood the full meaning of
the phrase until he read those words, "Sheen beat Peteiro".

There was no mistake about it. There the thing was. It
was impossible for the *Sportsman* to have been hoaxed. No,
the incredible, outrageous fact must be faced. Sheen had
been down to Aldershot and won a silver medal! Sheen!

Sheen!! Sheen who had—who was—well, who, in a word, was SHEEN!!!

Linton read on like one in a dream.

"The Light-Weights fell," said the writer, "to a newcomer Sheen, of Wrykyn" (Sheen!), "a clever youngster with a strong defence and a beautiful straight left, doubtless the result of tuition from the middle-weight ex-champion, Joe Bevan, who was in his corner for the final bout. None of his opponents gave him much trouble except Peteiro of Ripton, whom he met in the final. A very game and determined fight was seen when these two met, but Sheen's skill and condition discounted the rushing tactics of his adversary, and in the last minute of the third round the referee stopped the encounter." (Game and determined! Sheen!!) "Sympathy was freely expressed for Peteiro, who has thus been runner-up two years in succession. He, however, met a better man, and paid the penalty. The admirable pluck with which Sheen bore his punishment and gradually wore his man down made his victory the most popular of the day's programme."

Well!

Details of the fighting described Sheen as "cutting out the work". "popping in several nice lefts", "swinging his right for the point", and executing numerous other incredible manoeuvres.

Sheen!

You caught the name correctly? SHEEN, I'll trouble you.

Linton stared blankly across the school grounds. Then he burst into a sudden yell of laughter.

On that very morning the senior day-room was going to court-martial Sheen for disgracing the house. The resolution had been passed on the previous afternoon, probably just as he was putting the finishing touches to the "most popular victory of the day's programme". "This," said Linton, "is rich."

He grubbed a little hole in one of Mr Seymour's flower-beds, and laid the *Sportsman* to rest in it. The news would be about the school at nine o'clock, but if he could keep it from the senior day-room till the brief interval between breakfast and school, all would be well, and he would have the pure pleasure of seeing that backbone of the house make a complete ass of itself. A thought struck him. He unearthed the *Sportsman*, and put it in his pocket.

He strolled into the senior day-room after breakfast.

"Any one seen the *Sporter* this morning?" he inquired.

No one had seen it.

"The thing hasn't come," said some one.

"Good!" said Linton to himself.

At this point Stanning strolled into the room. "I'm a witness," he said, in answer to Linton's look of inquiry. "We're doing this thing in style. I depose that I saw the prisoner cutting off on the—whatever day it was, when he ought to have been saving our lives from the fury of the mob. Hadn't somebody better bring the prisoner into the dock?"

"I'll go," said Linton promptly. "I may be a little time, but don't get worried. I'll bring him all right."

He went upstairs to Sheen's study, feeling like an *impresario* about to produce a new play which is sure to create a sensation.

Sheen was in. There was a ridge of purple under his left eye, but he was otherwise intact.

" 'Gratulate you, Sheen," said Linton.

For an instant Sheen hesitated. He had rehearsed this kind of scene in his mind, and sometimes he saw himself playing a genial, forgiving, let's-say-no-more-about-it-we-all-make-mistakes-but-in-future! role, sometimes being cold haughty, and distant, and repelling friendly advances with icy disdain. If anybody but Linton had been the first to congratulate him he might have decided on this second line of action. But he liked Linton, and wanted to be friendly with him.

"Thanks," he said.

Linton sat down on the table and burst into a torrent of speech.

"You *are* a man! What did you want to do it for? Where the dickens did you learn to box? And why on earth, if you can win silver medals at Aldershot, didn't you

box for the house and smash up that sidey ass Stanning?
I say, look here, I suppose we haven't been making idiots
of ourselves all the time, have we?"

"I shouldn't wonder," said Sheen. "How?"

"I mean, you did— What I mean to say is— Oh, hang
it, *you* know! You did cut off when we had that row in the
town, didn't you?"

"Yes," said Sheen, "I did."

With that medal in his pocket it cost him no effort to
make the confession.

"I'm glad of that. I mean, I'm glad we haven't been such
fools as we might have been. You see, we only had Stan-
nings word to go on."

Sheen started.

"Stanning!" he said. "What do you mean?"

"He was the chap who started the story. Didn't you
know? He told everybody."

"I thought it was Drummond," said Sheen blankly. "You
remember meeting me outside his study the day after? I
thought he told you then."

"Drummond! Not a bit of it. He swore you hadn't been
with him at all. He was as sick as anything when I said I
thought I'd seen you with him."

"I—" Sheen stopped. "I wish I'd known," he concluded.
Then, after a pause, "So it was Stanning!"

"Yes,—conceited beast. Oh. I say."

"Um?"

"I see it all now. Joe Bevan taught you to box."

"Yes."

"Then that's how you came to be at the 'Blue Boar' that
day. He's the Bevan who runs it."

"That's his brother. He's got a gymnasium up at the top.
I used to go there every day."

"But I say, Great Scott, what are you going to do about
that?"

"How do you mean?"

"Why, Spence is sure to ask you who taught you to box.
He must know you didn't learn with the instructor. Then

it'll all come out, and you'll get dropped on for going up the river and going to the pub."

"Perhaps he won't ask," said Sheen.

"Hope not. Oh, by the way—"

"What's up?"

"Just remembered what I came up for. It's an awful rag. The senior day-room are going to court-martial you."

"Court-martial me!"

"For funking. They don't know about Aldershot, not a word. I bagged the *Sportsman* early, and hid it. They are going to get the surprise of their lifetime. I said I'd come up and fetch you."

"I shan't go." said Sheen.

Linton looked alarmed.

"Oh, but I say, you must. Don't spoil the thing. Can't you see what a rag it'll be?"

"I'm not going to sweat downstairs for the benefit of the senior day-room."

"I say," said Linton, "Stanning's there."

"What!"

"He's a witness," said Linton, grinning.

Sheen got up.

"Come on," he said.

Linton came on.

Down in the senior day-room the court was patiently awaiting the prisoner. Eager anticipation was stamped on its expressive features.

"Beastly time he is," said Clayton. Clayton was acting as president.

"We shall have to buck up," said Stanning. "Hullo, here he is at last. Come in, Linton."

"I was going to," said Linton, "but thanks all the same. Come along, Sheen."

"Shut that door, Linton," said Stanning from his seat on the table.

"All right, Stanning," said Linton. "Anything to oblige. Shall I bring up a chair for you to rest your feet on?"

"Forge ahead, Clayton," said Stanning to the president.

The president opened the court-martial in unofficial phraseology.

"Look here, Sheen," he said, "we've come to the conclusion that this has got a bit too thick."

"You mustn't talk in that chatty way, Clayton," interrupted Linton. " 'Prisoner at the bar's' the right expression to use. Why don't you let somebody else have a look in? You're the rottenest president of a court-martial I ever saw."

"Don't rag, Linton," said Clayton, with an austere frown. "This is serious."

"Glad you told me," said Linton. "Go on."

"Can't you sit down, Linton!" said Stanning.

"I was only waiting for leave. Thanks. You were saying something, Clayton. It sounded pretty average rot, but you'd better unburden your soul."

The president resumed.

"We want to know if you've anything to say—"

"You don't give him a chance," said Linton. "You bag the conversation so."

"—about disgracing the house."

"By getting the Gotford, you know, Sheen," explained Linton. "Clayton thinks that work's a bad habit, and ought to be discouraged."

Clayton glared, and looked at Stanning. He was not equal to the task of tackling Linton himself.

Stanning interposed.

"Don't rot, Linton. We haven't much time as it is."

"Sorry," said Linton.

"You've let the house down awfully," said Clayton.

"Yes?" said Sheen.

Linton took the paper out of his pocket, and smoothed it out.

"Seen the *Sporter*?" he asked casually. His neighbour grabbed at it.

"I thought it hadn't come," he said.

"Good account of Aldershot," said Linton.

He leaned back in his chair as two or three of the senior day-room collected round the *Sportsman*.

"Hullo! We won the gym.!"

"Rot! Let's have a look!"

This tremendous announcement quite eclipsed the court-martial as an object of popular interest. The senior day-room surged round the holder of the paper.

"Give us a chance," he protested.

"We can't have. Where is it? Biddle and Smith are simply hopeless. How the dickens can they have got the shield?"

"What a goat you are!" said a voice reproachfully to the possessor of the paper. "Look at this. It says Cheltenham got it. And here we are—seventeenth. Fat lot of shield we've won."

"Then what the deuce does this mean? 'Honours for St Paul's, Harrow, and Wrykyn'."

"Perhaps it refers to the boxing," suggested Linton.

"But we didn't send any one up. Look here. Harrow won the Heavies. St Paul's got the Middles. *Hullo!*"

"Great Scott!" said the senior day-room.

There was a blank silence. Linton whistled softly to himself.

The gaze of the senior day-room was concentrated on that ridge of purple beneath Sheen's left eye.

Clayton was the first to speak. For some time he had been waiting for sufficient silence to enable him to proceed with his presidential duties. He addressed himself to Sheen.

"Look here, Sheen," he said, "we want to know what you've got to say for yourself. You go disgracing the house—"

The stunned senior day-room were roused to speech.

"Oh, chuck it, Clayton."

"Don't be a fool, Clayton."

"Silly idiot!"

Clayton looked round in pained surprise at this sudden withdrawal of popular support.

"You'd better be polite to Sheen," said Linton; "he won the Light-Weights at Aldershot yesterday."

The silence once more became strained

"Well," said Sheen, "weren't you going to court-martial

me, or something? Clayton, weren't you saying something?"

Clayton started. He had not yet grasped the situation entirely; but he realised dimly that by some miracle Sheen had turned in an instant into a most formidable person.

"Er—no," he said. "No, nothing."

"The thing seems to have fallen through, Sheen," said Linton. "Great pity. Started so well, too. Clayton always makes a mess of things."

"Then I'd just like to say one thing," said Sheen.

Respectful attention from the senior day-room.

"I only want to know why you can't manage things of this sort by yourselves, without dragging in men from other houses."

"Especially men like Stanning," said Linton. "The same thing occurred to me. It's lucky Drummond wasn't here. Remember the last time, you chaps?"

The chaps did. Stanning became an object of critical interest. After all, who *was* Stanning? What right had he to come and sit on tables in Seymour's and interfere with the affairs of the house?

The allusion to "last time" was lost upon Sheen, but he saw that it had not improved Stanning's position with the spectators.

He opened the door.

"Good bye, Stanning," he said.

"If I hadn't hurt my wrist—" Stanning began.

"Hurt your wrist!" said Sheen. "You got a bad attack of Peteiro. That was what was the matter with you."

"You think that every one's a funk like yourself," said Stanning.

"Pity they aren't," said Linton; "we should do rather well down at Aldershot. And he wasn't such a terror after all, Sheen, was he? You beat him in two and a half rounds, didn't you? Think what Stanning might have done if only he hadn't sprained his poor wrist just in time.

"Look here, Linton—"

"Some are born with sprained wrists," continued the speaker, "some achieve sprained wrists—like Stanning—"

Stanning took a step towards him.

"Don't forget you've a sprained wrist," said Linton.

"Come on, Stanning," said Sheen, who was still holding the door open, "you'll be much more comfortable in your own house. I'll show you out."

"I suppose," said Stanning in the passage, "you think you've scored off me."

"That," said Sheen pleasantly, "is rather the idea. Good bye."

XXIV

BRUCE EXPLAINS

Mr Spence was a master with a great deal of sympathy and a highly developed sense of duty. It was the combination of these two qualities which made it so difficult for him to determine on a suitable course of action in relation to Sheen's out-of-bounds exploits. As a private individual he had nothing but admiration for the sporting way in which Sheen had fought his up-hill fight. He felt that he himself in similar circumstances would have broken any number of school rules. But, as a master, it was his duty, he considered, to report him. If a master ignored a breach of rules in one case, with which he happened to sympathise, he would in common fairness be compelled to overlook a similar breach of rules in other cases, even if he did not sympathise with them. In which event he would be of small use as a master.

On the other hand, Sheen's case was so exceptional that he might very well compromise to a certain extent between the claims of sympathy and those of duty. If he were to go to the headmaster and state baldly that Sheen had been in the habit for the last half-term of visiting an up-river public-house, the headmaster would get an entirely wrong idea of the matter, and suspect all sorts of things which had no existence in fact. When a boy is accused of frequenting a public-house, the head-magisterial mind leaps naturally to Stale Fumes and the Drunken Stagger.

So Mr Spence decided on a compromise. He sent for Sheen, and having congratulated him warmly on his victory in the Light-Weights, proceeded as follows :

"You have given me to understand, Sheen, that you were taught boxing by Bevan ?"

"Yes, sir."

"At the 'Blue Boar' ?"

"Yes, sir."

"This puts me in a rather difficult position, Sheen. Much as I dislike doing it, I am afraid I shall have to report this matter to the headmaster."

Sheen said he supposed so. He saw Mr Spence's point.

"But I shall not mention the 'Blue Boar'. If I did, the headmaster might get quite the wrong impression. He would not understand all the circumstances. So I shall simply mention that you broke bounds by going up the river. I shall tell him the whole story, you understand, and it's quite possible that you will hear no more of the affair. I'm sure I hope so. But you understand my position?"

"Yes, sir."

"That's all, then, Sheen. Oh, by the way, you wouldn't care for a game of fives before breakfast tomorrow, I suppose?"

"I should like it, sir."

"Not too stiff?"

"No, sir."

"Very well, then. I'll be there by a quarter-past seven."

Jack Bruce was waiting to see the headmaster in his study at the end of afternoon school.

"Well, Bruce," said the headmaster, coming into the room and laying down some books on the table, "do you want to speak to me? Will you give your father my congratulations on his victory. I shall be writing to him tonight. I see from the paper that the polling was very even. Apparently one or two voters arrived at the last moment and turned the scale."

"Yes, sir."

"It is a most gratifying result. I am sure that, apart from our political views, we should all have been disappointed if your father had not won. Please congratulate him sincerely."

"Yes, sir."

"Well, Bruce, and what was it that you wished to see me about?"

Bruce was about to reply when the door opened, and Mr Spence came in.

"One moment, Bruce," said the headmaster. "Yes, Spence?"

Mr Spence made his report clearly and concisely. Bruce listened with interest. He thought it hardly playing the game for the gymnasium master to hand Sheen over to be executed at the very moment when the school was shaking hands with itself over the one decent thing that had been done for it in the course of the athletic year; but he told himself philosophically that he supposed masters had to do these things. Then he noticed with some surprise that Mr Spence was putting the matter in a very favourable light for the accused. He was avoiding with some care any mention of the "Blue Boar". When he had occasion to refer to the scene of Sheen's training, he mentioned it vaguely as a house.

"This man Bevan, who is an excellent fellow and a personal friend of my own, has a house some way up the river."

Of course a public-house *is* a house.

"Up the river," said the headmaster meditatively.

It seemed that that was all that was wrong. The prosecution centred round that point, and no other. Jack Bruce, as he listened, saw his way of coping with the situation.

"Thank you, Spence," said the headmaster at the conclusion of the narrative. "I quite understand that Sheen's conduct was very excusable. But—I distinctly said—I placed the upper river out of bounds ... Well, I will see Sheen, and speak to him. I will speak to him."

Mr Spence left the room.

"Please sir—" said Jack Bruce.

"Ah, Bruce. I am afraid I have kept you some little time. Yes?

"I couldn't help hearing what Mr Spence was saying to you about Sheen, sir. I don't think he knows quite what really happened."

"You mean—?"

"Sheen went there by road. I used to take him in my motor."

"Your—! What did you say, Bruce?"

"My motor-car, sir. That's to say, my father's. We used to go together every day."

"I am glad to hear it. I am glad. Then I need say nothing to Sheen after all. I am glad . . . But—er—Bruce," proceeded the headmaster after a pause.

"Yes, sir?"

"Do you—are you in the habit of driving a motor-car frequently?"

"Every day, sir. You see, I am going to take up motors when I leave school, so it's all education."

The headmaster was silent. To him the word "Education" meant Classics. There was a Modern side at Wrykyn, and an Engineering side, and also a Science side; but in his heart he recognised but one Education—the Classics. Nothing that he had heard, nothing that he had read in the papers and the monthly reviews had brought home to him the spirit of the age and the fact that Things were not as they used to be so clearly as this one remark of Jack Bruce's. For here was Bruce admitting that in his spare time he drove motors. And, stranger still, that he did it not as a wild frolic but seriously, with a view to his future career.

"The old order changeth," thought the headmaster a little sadly.

Then he brought himself back from his mental plunge into the future.

"Well, well, Bruce," he said, "we need not discuss the merits and demerits of driving motor-cars, need we? What did you wish to see me about?"

"I came to ask if I might get off morning school tomorrow, sir. Those voters who got to the poll just in time and settled the election—I brought them down in the car. And the policeman—he's a Radical, and voted for Pedder—Mr Pedder—has sworn—says I was exceeding the speed-limit."

The headmaster pressed a hand to his forehead, and his mind swam into the future.

"Well, Bruce?" he said at length, in the voice of one whom nothing can surprise now.

"He says I was going twenty-eight miles an hour. And if I can get to the Court tomorrow morning I can prove that I wasn't. I brought them to the poll in the little runabout."

"And the —er—little runabout," said the headmaster, "does not travel at twenty-eight miles an hour?"

"No, sir. It can't go more than twenty at the outside."

"Very well, Bruce, you need not come to school tomorrow morning."

"Thank you, sir."

The headmaster stood thinking . . . The new order . . .

"Bruce," he said.

"Yes, sir?"

"Tell me, do I look very old?"

Bruce stared.

"Do I look three hundred years old?"

"No, sir," said Bruce, with the stolid wariness of the boy who fears that a master is subtly chaffing him.

"I feel more, Bruce," said the headmaster, with a smile. "I feel more. You will remember to congratulate your father for me, won't you?"

Outside the door Jack Bruce paused in deep reflection. "Rum!" he said to himself. "Jolly rum!"

On the senior gravel he met Sheen.

"Hullo, Sheen," he said, "what are you going to do?"

"Drummond wants me to tea with him in the infirmary."

"It's all right, then?"

"Yes. I got a note from him during afternoon school. You coming?"

"All right. I say, Sheen, the Old Man's rather rum sometimes, isn't he?"

"What's he been doing now?"

"Oh—nothing. How do you feel after Aldershot? Tell us all about it. I've not heard a word yet."

AFTERWORD

It is natural for a young writer to turn to his own youth for his first stories. For in the first place, he doesn't yet know of very much else, and in the second, childhood has always a compulsive fascination to us all. But what makes English writers rather different from those of other countries, is that their boy or girlhood stories are so often set in schools.

For most European or American writers don't seem to have thought of their schools as interesting places: the only exception I can think of is Alain Fournier's *Le Grand Meaulnes*. Or if they wrote of schooldays at all, it was to describe how horrible they were, as in Jules Renard's *Poil de Carotte*. True, some English writers have also shuddered at their memories of the dear old college, and Dickens's Dotheboys Hall has become a legendary place of infant woe. But mostly school books, from *Tom Brown's Schooldays* onwards, evoke distant boyhood through a hazy glow of adulation.

So, in setting his early tales in imaginary colleges, the young P. G. Wodehouse was employing what was, by the early 1900s, already a well-tried literary form. He may also have realised, instinctively, that a school setting has other great advantages to a young writer. The first is that, like Shakespeare's palaces or Joseph Conrad's ships, a school is a little world all of its own, so that a book about one has its form all ready made, without the writer's having to invent one. A school also has its almost predictable cast of characters: a god-like headmaster, other teachers splendid or comical, the good boys, the bad boys, the exotics and the eccentrics. There are also—except, perhaps, for a remote Matron and the headmaster's young daughter—few female roles to bother about, and since young male writers often find these difficult to handle, a school tale gives them a splendid reason for not introducing any girls at all.

Then there is another advantage, which Mr Wodehouse, being a shrewd man, surely recognised; which is that boys are great readers and, as with all of us, what people most like reading about, is themselves; so that with school tales,

not only the writer's subject, but his public, are both
assured. And more than this; so firmly fixated do so many
English adults seem to be on their glorious schooldays, that
books about schools have a large adult readership as well;
and this was specially so half a century ago, when detective
stories, or crime and spy tales—let alone science fiction—
had not yet come to claim the attention of dignified adults
beneath whose ample waistcoats there still beat the young
heart of a boy.

The school P. G. Wodehouse went to was Dulwich
College, in south London—an excellent day-school founded
by Edward Alleyn, the Elizabethan actor; and Dulwich
has the enormous distinction of having, among its illustri-
ous alumni, not only Mr Wodehouse himself but the late
great Raymond Chandler. In Mr Wodehouse's day,
Dulwich, now overgrown almost completely, was still a
semi-rural locality, so that the College had something of
the atmosphere of a country school.

This may be one reason why P. G. Wodehouse set his
own school stories not in urban day, but in rural boarding
schools. Another reason may be that this is the traditional
setting for school stories—partly, perhaps, because boarding schools are considered more distinguished than day
schools, but also, certainly, because an isolated college
provides a more perfect setting—rather like a desert island
—for the peculiar goings-on that, in school stories, always
seem to occur from the first page to the last.

However, Mr Wodehouse being Mr Wodehouse, the
schools of these tales are not quite like any others in the
scholarly, or literary, canons; and it is fascinating to observe,
as one reads them, how the young P.G.W. is already practising so many of the technical and comical stratagems that
he was later to perfect in such settings as Blandings castle,
or Bertie Wooster's celebrated Mayfair flat.

We may first notice that P. G. Wodehouse always had
that most valuable of story-teller's gifts, which is a capacity
to entertain. When most strangers button-hole us in real
life, we retreat from them in dismay, for we know to our
cost that so many racconteurs are bores. But from time to

time an interlocutor confronts us who, like the Ancient Mariner, has the gift of halting us in our tracks and bewitching us to listen. This gift is outstanding in P. G. Wodehouse's art, and these books reveal that he possessed its secret from the outset.

The next quality we note is that while Mr Wodehouse is, and always was, a remarkably shrewd man—one far, far wiser in the ways of the wicked world than he may at first appear to be—he has also seemed to possess and, more extraordinarily, never to have lost as he grew older and more experienced, a sort of glorious, primal innocence. By this I do not at all mean that he was ever simply naive: far from it, and indeed, in the terrible century we live in, no one any longer has the right to be wilfully unknowing. But innocence is a rarer, deeper, and more splendid blessing: the wise innocence of Candide, or of the saintly simple-hearted whose pure natures shine out from the frightening pages of Dostoievsky. "Blessed are the pure in heart" can be said of so few writers—of Tchehov, perhaps, and certainly of P. G. Wodehouse.

We may then observe how brilliantly he could juggle, even at this early age, with a complicated plot, and a considerable, and varied cast list. A good exercise, once you've finished a book by Mr Wodehouse, is to see if you can explain the plot to someone else, and who the principal characters are, and what they did. This turns out to be as impossible as trying to do the same with *Hamlet*: for although the play seems perfectly clear while one is watching it, in retrospect, one realises its enormous intricacy, and the skill with which the writer has made a fascinating complexity crystal-clear as he unfolds it to the audience or reader.

Students of the later novels must have noticed how fond Mr Wodehouse is of apt—if often ludicrous—quotation: Jeeves, for example, is fond of rebuking the wayward Bertie by some telling line culled from the Golden Treasury, and he often evokes "the poet Keats" or the holy writ of the Old Testament, to reinforce a stricture to his young master. Indeed, Mr Wodehouse must have been an attentive pupil himself at Dulwich College—at any rate, in the English and divinity classes. For already, in these books, pregnant quotes fall fast from surprising lips—in *A Prefect's Uncle*, I found Shakespeare, Kipling, W. S. Gilbert, the Legends Ingoldsby, Music Hall song, and *Tom Brown's Schooldays* themselves, quoted pertinently in the first half dozen chapters.

In this book we may also encounter what seems to be, and have become increasingly, a veritable obsession of Mr Wodehouse's : and that is, the terrible powers, over the defenceless male, of Aunts. Everyone remembers, from the Jeeves and Bertie saga, the benevolent Aunt Dahlia (with her wonderful French chef Anatole), and how he shudders at each appearance of the terrifying Aunt Agatha. Well, here we have not only several aunts, but even a schoolboy uncle who is four years younger than the book's embarrassed hero : whom this appalling infant treats—despite his older nephew's being a top lad of the academy—with maddening condescension.

In *William Tell Told Again*, P. G. Wodehouse turns schoolmaster himself, and he relates, with enormous gusto and enjoyment, this famous tale of the Swiss hero, and the wicked Austrians he finally overthrows. Mr Wodehouse, would, I feel, have made an excellent school teacher himself, for he knows how to see the world as boys do—a gift we all think we have, but in reality soon lose; and in fact, his only defect, had he become a dominie, would have been his giving us perpetual half-holidays, and taking us off to play cricket—or even Out of Bounds, into the wicked village that always seems to nestle three miles or so from the Old Grey Walls of the dear old School.

William Tell was, as a matter of fact, the first book of Mr Wodehouse's that I read myself—and at the perfect age, for I was then a schoolboy; and I remember vividly how engaging and delightful I found his story, and so unlike the "history" crammed with meaningless dates and battles that they forced on me at school. What I most felt, I think, was that the author was my friend, my ally; whereas most adult writers seemed to be telling me to do what I didn't want to, or not do what I did.

I have already said elsewhere that I believe P. G. Wodehouse to be the finest living writer of English prose; and although there may be more who share this view today than did in earlier decades, I think one reason why so many readers—and even dedicated fans—have not spotted how gifted he really is, is that, being an exquisitely courteous writer, he always makes it seem so easy to the reader. He's like a magician, really : look, no hands ! But behind this seemingly effortless performance there is infinite skill, and a splendid, kindly wisdom; and in these early books, we can observe the young Wodehouse learning how to enchant us with these two rare and beautiful gifts.

COLIN MACINNES
Davis-Poynter Ltd
Broadwick House & Street
WIV 2

April 1972